RAINBOW GOLD

Looking for love, Georgina flirted with any man who gave her a second glance . . . every man, in fact, but the one who seemed beyond her reach. She played with fire until he came into her life and then she drew back from the flame that was Bart Blair — but she was badly burned just the same and her heart would carry the scars for ever.

JULIET GRAY

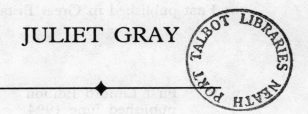

RAINBOW GOLD

Complete and Unabridged

LINFORD
Leicester

First published in Great Britain

First Linford Edition
published June 1994

British Library CIP Data

Gray, Juliet
  Rainbow gold.—Large print ed.—
  Linford romance library
  I. Title II. Series
  823.914 [F]

  ISBN 0-7089-7541-0

Published by
F. A. Thorpe (Publishing) Ltd.
Anstey, Leicestershire
Set by Words & Graphics Ltd.
Anstey, Leicestershire
Printed and bound in Great Britain by
T. J. Press (Padstow) Ltd., Padstow, Cornwall

This book is printed on acid-free paper

1

GEORGINA hurried across the cobbled court, passed through the high, narrow arch of the shabby mansions and turned into the busy thoroughfare with its throng of people, constant flow of traffic and sprinkling of famous theatres.

The rain was bouncing back from the wet pavements and strangers turned to look at the trim young woman in the bright orange raincoat and matching, wide-brimmed rainhat. She was a colourful and very attractive sight on a dull grey morning. To many people she was also a familiar figure in that small corner of London's Theatreland. Shopkeepers waved and smiled, the paper-seller on the corner greeted her with all the familiarity of an old friend and the policeman on point duty at the busy traffic lights, where the buses

1

and taxis and vans always seemed to be snarled up at this hour of the working day, winked at her in friendly fashion and stopped the traffic with a flourish so that she could cross in safety.

Not only Georgina, of course . . . but she hurried across, feeling like a celebrity, and turned to wave her thanks as she reached the opposite pavement. A little amused, she went on her way, quickening her steps for she was later than usual and there was probably a great deal of work waiting on her desk. Fortunately the *Elysium* was only a stone's throw from her tiny but comfortable flat.

She reached the front of the theatre and ran up the wide steps to push her way through one of the heavy glass doors. Usually she turned down the alley beside the theatre and entered by the stage door which gave easy access to the private flight of stairs leading to the offices. This morning, she wanted to save a few moments and speak to the house manager on her way through.

Cleaners were busy in the foyer with hoovers and dusters. Georgina exchanged smiles and friendly greetings and paused to ask after the sick grandchild of one of the women with genuine interest. She was a warm and friendly person, much-liked and very popular, and not only because of her interest in everyone and everything about her. She was extremely pretty with shining, blonde hair that danced on her shoulders, clear grey eyes that were friendly and direct, a swift and sunny smile that could endear her to a stranger in a moment and an enchanting, heart-shaped face with its slender nose, generous and very sweet mouth and fresh, clear complexion.

Her lovely smile had absolutely no impact on the man who glanced up from the morning mail with a frown as she entered the office. Bartholomew Blair was not the easiest of men. As actor-manager of a very successful theatre that had so far resisted all the lures of the big entertainment

3

combines, he was a busy man, a demanding man who did not suffer fools gladly, a man who insisted on perfection from his company and his staff. He knew, of course, that perfection was impossible but it kept everyone on their toes trying to attain it!

"Remind me to buy you an efficient alarm clock for Christmas," he said dryly.

Georgina's smile widened. "Generous!" she exclaimed.

"It is," he agreed grimly. "I buy very few Christmas presents." He held out a sheaf of letters. "These are routine . . . I'll go through the others with you later." He glanced pointedly at his watch. "I'm expecting Stuart in ten minutes . . . there isn't time now to get involved with the mail."

"I am late . . . but not as late as it seems," she said firmly. "I've been with Marshall for some time."

He nodded. "Box office receipts?"

"Up a little . . . that's good, isn't it?"

4

She smiled encouragingly, wondering exactly what had put him into a difficult mood. He was seldom bubbling with *joie de vivre* at this hour of the day but he was not always so grim.

"How are the advance bookings?"

She went to her desk and looked up the appropriate figures. "Not doing too well," she admitted ruefully.

"No . . . the critics slammed it too hard," he said wryly. "Do you know, I rather think I was persuaded against my better judgement to put on this play."

Georgina was silent but a little colour stole into her face. No one could fairly describe her part in the matter as persuasion but she had certainly encouraged him to read the script that had lain unheeded on his desk for two weeks after she quietly placed it there. The playwright was a friend from her RADA days and she had promised to bring his work to Bart Blair's notice. Her employer had eventually read the play, pronounced it raw but promising and set it to one side. In the months that followed Georgina had gently reminded him of its existence from time to time and lightly hinted at her own faith in its future. Bart had finally decided to put it on and spent long and weary hours working with Stuart to polish its rougher edges. It had opened two weeks before and the critics had disliked it to a man. But Georgina still felt that the play had something and it was particularly well-cast and she believed that the tide of public approval must turn if its run continued for a few more weeks. But it was losing money and she suspected that the curtain would soon fall for the last time on *Devil's Delight*.

"It's a damn good play," he said unexpectedly. "For my part, it deserves a fair crack of the whip . . . we'll give it another week." He had made up his mind to tell Stuart that very morning that the play must come off . . . he did not know what had caused him to alter that decision. Certainly not his secretary's friendship with the young man although he was well aware that Georgina would be disappointed by the play's failure. Perhaps his own deep-rooted conviction that the critics were mistaken . . . and not for the first time in the history of the theatre.

Georgina's heart-shaped face was suddenly aglow. Bart looked down at her, wondering that it obviously meant so much that Webb's play should not fail. Unexpectedly warmed and slightly disconcerted by the radiance in her smile, he turned away and went into his own office, leaving the door open as he always did unless he wished for privacy. A closed door meant that he must not be disturbed.

Georgina bent her blonde head dutifully over the mail and Bart studied her thoughtfully while he waited for the young man he had chosen to back with so far disastrous results. His secretary and Stuart Webb were friends but he did not know how involved they were with each other. Webb made no secret of his affection for Georgia, as he called her, but she seemed very light-hearted in her response. Sometimes it seemed to Bart, an impersonal onlooker, that there were too many men in her life. She always had one man or another in tow and he suspected that she liked variety too much to settle for a lasting relationship with any man.

He admitted her prettiness, her vivacity, her generous warmth of heart. He understood why she was so well-liked, so sought-after, but he did not care for her attitude bordering on indifference towards men or her deplorably fickle behaviour. In fact, he disapproved of her and sometimes it was difficult not to show it. However, she was an efficient secretary and her personal life was none of his concern. They saw little of each other outside working hours if he could avoid it for he disliked the thought of the gossip that might arise if he should be seen too often with his pretty secretary. But it was not always possible to avoid her for they had many friends in common.

Only last night, she had been with one of his friends, dancing till dawn at a famous club. It was scarcely surprising that she had overslept, he thought drily. He had been surprised to see her with Lucas Winfull . . . and on such friendly terms as his companion had taken pains to point out. A little smile suddenly tugged at his lips. Prudence clung to the ridiculous fancy that he had a certain *tendre* for Georgina Durrell and supposed he was unaware of her attempts to trap him into an involuntary, unconscious betrayal. Nothing could be further from the truth, of course. He did not admire Georgina's type at all . . . it was merely her typing that suited him so well!

Georgina looked up to see that faint smile about his mouth and thought idly how attractive he must appear to a woman when he chose to charm. Yet he was always firmly impersonal, even cool, where she was concerned — and she was thankful for it, knowing that it might be all too easy to warm to him and quite determined that love should not play a part in her life a second time. Once bitten, twice shy, she thought fiercely. No man should ever again be handed that particular stick to beat her with! *Love is a fool's game and the devil's delight* . . . the words from Stuart's play leaped to her mind and her heart surged passionately in agreement. A great many sins and follies were committed in the name of love, she thought bitterly. She had been a fool once but she would never again delight the devil by falling in love.

Play it cool! Keep it light! Safety in numbers! Adopting that approach, she had found that it worked. She had managed to forget pain and humiliation and recall only the lessons that loving had taught. Now she had friends that she did not allow to become lovers and she found it possible to like, to admire, even to grow fond without becoming so involved that anxiety crept in. It had taken time but now she was very sure that she could hold on to her heart.

Meeting Bartholomew Blair for the first time she had instantly recognised that he was the kind of man who constituted a real threat. For there was something about him that she had instinctively admired — a strength of character, an integrity, a discipline of mind and spirit that set him apart from and above most men that she knew. Yet she accepted the offered post as his secretary — and accepted the threat to her emotions that went with the job.

She had been working at the *Elysium* for some months and prided herself that she had successfully resisted all temptation to like Bart Blair too much for her own good. She admired him. She loved working for him and with him and she was glad that their mutual love for the theatre was a bond between them. But they were very much employer and secretary . . . and Georgina was thankful. He was the kind of man she might have loved, she admitted honestly — and she never wanted to love again. She had been torn to pieces by loving and she was still trying to put herself together again . . .

She had loved with all the intensity of her youth and innocence, desperately caught in the whirlpool of new and overwhelming emotion. He had been older, experienced, knowing women and how to kindle their emotions to his advantage — and she had foolishly supposed that he loved her and meant to marry her and her heart had felt that it must explode with happiness.

Youthfully, impetuously generous in love, she had gladly given herself when weeks of subtle persuasion had finally brought her to the verge of surrender. She had lain in his arms and talked confidently of a golden future . . . how wonderful it would be, how happy she would make him, how much they would always love each other. He had held her in careless embrace, murmuring drowsy agreement, scarcely attending until she uttered the one word that instantly alerted his instinct for self-preservation.

She mentioned marriage — and that was no part of his plan and he did not hesitate to say so. Shocked, sick with dismay, she had stumbled out a reminder of his claim to love her . . . and he had laughed.

For someone like Georgina, it was the end — and he had swiftly made it clear that it was the end, anyway. Later, she understood that it was the chase and not the capture that excited and held his interest . . . he was that kind of man. She could not remain at RADA and see him in hot pursuit of the next unsuspecting victim. She could not endure the silent sympathy of friends and the not-so-silent scorn of the few who regarded her with hostility because she was pretty and popular and came from a famous theatrical family. For some time, she had been aware that love for the theatre, a desire to succeed and a burning ambition to follow the family tradition could not really take the place of talent. She was not a very good actress and all the training in the world would not turn her into one, she sensibly decided and left RADA to take a secretarial course, thinking that she might at least be of use to her mother who had retired from the theatre to become a successful novelist.

After all, Georgina had decided against leaving London and her many friends and the tiny flat that was so convenient and so ridiculously cheap and situated in the very heart of Theatreland. For some time she worked for an agency that specialised in supplying temporary office staff. The past had left its mark and she was reluctant to commit herself to anything too permanent, whether it be a job or a personal relationship.

Pure chance had taken her to the *Elysium* as temporary replacement for the elderly secretary who was finally forced to concede that a raging headache and high fever were not conducive to taking shorthand notes and transcribing them with accuracy.

It had been a very interesting and enjoyable week that Georgina had spent with Bartholomew Blair once she discovered that one could forgive him almost anything in return for a quiet word of approval or one of the enchanting but extremely rare smiles that transformed his harsh features. She left with a pang of regret when his secretary came back — and found that every other temporary job she took in the following weeks was boring and frustrating.

She had made new friends in that brief week at the *Elysium* but she had not supposed that Bart Blair was among them so she was surprised and pleased and foolishly flattered when he wrote to offer her a permanent position. She promptly telephoned to accept, perhaps a little too promptly, for he went to lengths to impress on her without actually saying so that he had no personal motive for offering her the job. Georgina had swiftly grasped that he merely appreciated her intelligence and efficiency, her understanding of the theatre and its demands, and felt that her particular background would make her a valuable addition to his staff . . . and the cold-blooded assessment had suited her very well.

For several months they had worked together in quiet harmony. Bart was impersonal, keeping her lightly but decidedly at a distance, almost but not quite a friend and always an employer. Georgina was glad that there were no emotional complications to a job that she thoroughly enjoyed and would hate to lose. He could be difficult and demanding, often infuriating, sometimes cold enough to chill the warmest nature. But he was a brilliant man of the theatre and it was easy to overlook his faults and impossible not to admire and respect him.

Stuart Webb arrived to be welcomed with a warmth that disconcerted him for he had been sure that the summons to Bart Blair's office must mean bad news. Georgina ushered him into the inner sanctum and her warm, reassuring smile together with the readiness with which Bart rose to offer his hand sent his volatile spirits soaring. He gripped the hand of the man who had shown so much kindly interest in his work and spent so much time and energy to help him achieve a polished play that deserved better than it had so far received from critics and public alike. "You're not taking it off!" he exclaimed thankfully, betraying the anxiety that had beset his every waking moment in the past few days.

Bart looked at him with a sardonic gleam in his very blue eyes. "Optimism runs in the veins of every playwright," he said drily. He swung his chair slightly towards the wide window that provided a panoramic view of London's roof-tops. "There are thousands of people out there who ought to be booking seats for this play of yours," he declared. "But they stay away and we would be playing to a virtually empty theatre if it wasn't for all the 'paper' we distribute. We're losing money, my friend."

Stuart went white. So it was the chop, after all, he thought miserably . . . no more than he had expected but none the easier to accept for all that. He mustered a vestige of a smile. "At least you gave me a chance," he said with quiet dignity, doing his best to swallow his disappointment. "I'll always be grateful for that, Sir Bartholomew."

Bart looked at him steadily for a moment. Then he smiled . . . that rare, rich smile that utterly redeemed the rather harsh features and slightly forbidding expression. "I believe in you and your work," he said firmly. "Your writing has all the right ingredients for success. This particular play may be a little too off-beat for Mr. Average but it isn't a bad play by any means. It could still break even . . . could possibly make money despite a bad beginning. So it will continue to run while I invest in a great deal of the right kind of publicity. I think the advance bookings will look more encouraging within a few days."

Stuart sat down rather suddenly. "I don't know what to say . . . " he began shakily.

"Say nothing if you mean to stick *Sir Bartholomew* at the end of it," Bart told him drily. He buzzed for Georgina and when she put her head around the door, he smiled and said lightly: "Could we have some coffee? We'll drink to the health of *Devil's Delight* and hope that it takes a turn for the better!"

"I'll drink to that!" she replied warmly . . . and Stuart sent her a warm little smile that implied he knew whom to thank for the reprieve. He was quite mistaken, of course, thought Georgina as she went away to make the coffee . . . she had no influence whatsoever over Bart's decisions. But it was surprising how many people seemed to think that they had only to win the secretary's approval to get what they wanted from the boss! In this particular case, she supposed it was natural that Stuart should feel that she had played some part in his success for she had brought this play to Bart's notice. But only because she had been so sure that it was a good play and merited a chance . . .

2

WHEN Georgina returned with the coffee that she had brewed in the little kitchen of the flat that few people knew to exist at the very top of the theatre and that was Bart's very private domain, she found the door of his office firmly closed . . . the sign that he did not wish to be disturbed.

She also found Prudence Carroll in the outer office, perched on the edge of the desk, swinging her lovely legs and glancing idly through the scrapbook of old theatre programmes that contained all the long history of the *Elysium*.

Prudence was a vision of loveliness. The cloud of auburn hair framed a perfect oval face. Her sparkling green eyes were fringed with the thickest and longest of dark lashes, entirely her own. Her features appeared to be delicately carved from warm ivory. Her beautiful body brought a natural elegance to anything and everything she wore. She had a deliciously husky voice, an enchanting smile, a delightful personality and very little conceit. She was warm-hearted and good-natured and seemed to be wholly lacking in the temperament that was usually found in the famous.

She was really too good to be true, Georgina always felt, needing some reason, however unsupported, for her vague dislike and distrust of the woman.

The warm beauty was quite flawless and made Georgina feel snub-nosed, large-mouthed and positively plain. Her movements conveyed a grace that must convince all other women of their own awkwardness. She was dressed by the most expensive couturiers of London, Paris and New York — and conveyed the impression that she would look just as fabulous in a cotton frock from a chain store. The quiet elegance always made Georgina feel that her own clothes were either too flamboyant or too dowdy but never quite right. And Prudence possessed a supreme self-assurance that was inborn rather than acquired and managed to reduce Georgina to a feeling of insignificant inferiority without even trying.

As a result, Georgina was usually on the defensive when they met and now she nodded, coolly, as Prudence greeted her with an easy, disarmingly friendly smile. "Coffee, is it? How lovely! May I have some . . . I'm parched in this heat," she declared in her lilting accents and with the ease of manner that did not expect rebuff.

"Yes, of course," Georgina poured the steaming, fragrant liquid into one of the delicate cups. She glanced briefly at the closed door of the inner office. "Does Bart know that you're here?" she asked lightly, deliberately using his first name. The intimacy thus implied brought her an odd little satisfaction although it was quite impossible to penetrate the armour of someone so very sure of her importance in a man's life as Prudence Carroll.

"No . . . he isn't expecting me and I didn't dare to disturb him," Prudence returned brightly. "Is he with someone very important? I'm off to the sunny South of France at the drop of a hat and just called in to let him know. We're finally about to start work on the new film after weeks of argy-bargy!"

"Lovely for you," Georgina said dutifully, knowing a slight twinge of envy at the thought of sun and sand and sea on the Riviera. The almost-tropical rain that morning had been the only break in a long spell of hot, dry weather and the sun had already broken through again with the promise of another very hot day and one sometimes longed to have nothing to do but laze and swim and enjoy the beautiful summer.

Prudence smiled wryly, reading the girl's mind. It was strange that so many people should assume that her life was one round of pleasure and luxury and completely overlooked the obvious fact that filming was extremely demanding and arduous, involving long hours and a wealth of patience. One had only to mention the South of France and Georgina Durrell, like almost everyone else, immediately visualised her as lying on the warm sand beneath blue skies and hot sun all day and every day and living it up in nightclubs and casinos half the night. Whereas work on the new film would absorb her so completely during each day that she would be too exhausted to do anything but retire to bed with a book at the end of the day.

"Lucky old me," she merely said lightly, knowing it would be a waste of time to explain the real facts of the matter. "I'm hoping Bart will be able to fly out for a few days if he isn't too busy," she went on. "Is his calendar very crowded just now?"

"Well, we are having problems with the current production," Georgina said dampingly although she knew perfectly well that Bart would respond to the merest hint that Prudence wished for his company. However busy he might be, he always found time for Prudence.

"So he was saying last night," Prudence recalled. "We saw you, by the way . . . dancing cheek to cheek with Lucas Winfull," she went on without an ounce of malice. "He's nice, isn't he? I've always been very fond of Lucas . . . we're old friends."

Georgina was particularly sensitive to feline spite but she could not detect the least trace of it in the light words. "Very nice," she agreed, smiling. "Were you and Bart at the *El Cosa* . . . I'm afraid I didn't notice you."

"We were with friends and soon moved on to another place," Prudence explained. Her eyes twinkled. "Anyway, you only had eyes for Lucas — and who can blame you!"

The door of Bart's office opened abruptly. "What's happened to the coffee . . . ? Prudence! How nice! I didn't hope to see you today!"

Bart exclaimed warmly, covering the distance between them with swift strides and catching her slender hands in his own with every indication of delight.

Prudence lightly brushed his lean cheek with her lips. "Surprise for you, darling . . . I'm on my way to the airport — or ought to be! We're actually about to start shooting the new film!"

"Marvellous!" he said warmly, knowing that there had been many difficulties to overcome before work could actually begin on the film based on the life of Bartok in which she played a starring rôle. "Every little wrinkle finally ironed out?"

"Not quite but there have been too many delays. I gather that Jordan is beginning to come apart at the seams," she said wryly, mentioning the brilliant American who was to direct the film. "But you're busy, Bart . . . I've come at a bad moment," she added swiftly, glancing towards the young man who stood by Bart's desk with a script in his hand but his admiring eyes upon her.

"We're virtually through," Bart said firmly. "Come and be introduced to Stuart Webb . . . he'll be delighted to meet a fan. I've told him how much you liked the play and his ego needs a boost just now," he added, smiling. He ushered her into the office, turning to say lightly: "Georgina, cancel my appointments . . . I shall be going to the airport with Miss Carroll."

Georgina took in the heavy tray with the silver coffeepot and delicate china. Bart accepted his coffee with a brief nod of thanks. Stuart took his cup from her hand and forgot to thank her at all for she was completely cast into the shade just then by the glowing personality of the internationally famous film star. Prudence was assuring him that she had thoroughly enjoyed and understood *Devil's Delight* and totally disagreed with the critics and felt sure that the play would run for years . . . and Stuart was responding as would any young, hopeful playwright to such encouragement from a very gifted actress. Prudence was utterly sincere, of course . . . she never said anything that she did not mean wholeheartedly and that was one of the really nice things about the woman, Georgina admitted, not too grudgingly. She was genuinely interested in people and she had a natural, warm generosity that led her into impulsive friendships . . . such as the one she had recently begun with Rennie Bruce, Georgina thought, a little bitterly.

Rennie was doing very well since leaving RADA earlier in the year and he had won an important part in the film that starred Prudence Carroll . . . perhaps because he was an able actor but also perhaps because they had become close friends. And would become closer still, Georgina thought unhappily . . . they would be thrown together in the weeks to come and an affair was inevitable. For Prudence liked Rennie . . . she had made that very obvious. And the fact that she was virtually engaged to Bart would not prevent her from enjoying the attentions of the good-looking, personable and very charming Rennie who undoubtedly realised all the advantages of friendship with an influential star.

Georgina had no illusions about him . . . not any more. She knew that Rennie was only concerned with himself and would trample on his dearest friends to get what he wanted. But the bitter knowledge of all that was lacking in him did not automatically erase the way she felt about him. It was inevitable that they met occasionally, that they heard news of each other, for they were both connected with Theatreland and it was a small, intimate, gossipy world. She was pleased for his success but at the same time she was very bitter that she did not share it with him. The *might-have-been* was very much in her thoughts of late and so it was not surprising that she did not look very kindly on Prudence Carroll.

Thanking her for the coffee with a

little nod, Bart met her eyes and he discovered a slight impatience in the grey depths. He knew instinctively that it was directed against Prudence whom she so obviously did not like. It was no part of her contract that she must like the women in his life, of course. But it puzzled him a little for Prudence was universally liked by both men and women ... and he wondered if Georgina was being unconsciously perverse or if she had a valid reason for her dislike.

He did not think her present mood had anything to do with the fact that Stuart was falling over himself to impress the lovely Prudence although that could not please Georgina very much. He was inclined to believe that the whole thing stemmed from jealousy of another kind. Georgina had studied at RADA, he knew. She had never given him an explanation for her abrupt termination of a dramatic career but he suspected that the reality had not matched the dream. A girl with her particular background had probably hoped to be as brilliant as her father, as much-loved as her mother. The discovery that she would never make the grade might easily colour her attitude towards someone like Prudence, so gifted and successful, such a darling of the gods. The seeds of jealousy are in us all and it might be very natural for Georgina, still smarting from her RADA experiences, to dislike and resent an actress, little older than herself, who had won both fame and fortune in the theatre.

For himself, he was very proud of Prudence whom he had known for several years. They were very close and it seemed inevitable that they would marry one day but for the moment they made very few demands on each other. Their respective careers made more than enough demands and love and marriage took a very secondary place for the time being. Bart knew that Prudence loved him and he was content. She liked male company and responded instinctively to admiration and attention but he was very sure that she reserved her love for him. And she was the only woman of real importance in his life. Prudence knew and understood the brief and quite meaningless affairs that he enjoyed with other women and did not allow them to disturb her. He was free to live his life as he pleased . . . just as she was free to enjoy the attention and the company of other men if she wished.

Neither was ready for the ultimate commitment of marriage. Bart cherished his freedom and his independence, considered himself self-sufficient, felt that he was much too busy and much too involved with his work to give a wife the time and attention that she must merit. Prudence was gifted and very ambitious and she gave almost all of herself to her career — and Bart understood better than most that she belonged more to her public than to any man for the moment. He wanted her success almost as much as he wanted his own. She had always sought stardom and finally achieved it. His life revolved around the *Elysium* and his small contribution to the Arts and it seemed to him that marriage could never bring the thrill, the delight, the glow of happiness that he had felt on learning that he was to receive the royal accolade for his services to the theatre.

Sir Bartholomew Blair . . . it had a ring to it that pleased him although he refused to allow anyone to call him anything but Bart or Blair as they had always done. He was just a man and he was the first to point out that his success could not have been won without a responsible and reliable staff, clever playwrights, brilliant companies and all the hundred and one others who kept a theatre with its curtain raised, its seats filled and its doors open to a paying and appreciative public . . .

Prudence paused to touch Georgina lightly on the shoulder and murmur a brief, friendly farewell. She was always very pleasant to Bart's secretary as though she sensed an antagonism, was troubled by it and sought to eradicate it. Georgina was in the middle of making a telephone call, cancelling one of Bart's appointments, and she merely smiled and nodded and silently mouthed *Good luck*, referring to the new film.

Bart scribbled *Back by two* across an envelope and pushed it towards Georgina, turning immediately to tuck Prudence's hand tenderly into his arm and smile at her with that rich and enchanting smile as they went from the office. Stuart left with them, merely grinning and waggling his fingers in a careless wave for Georgina as he followed in their wake.

Georgina finished the call and replaced the receiver and drew a deep breath, feeling the stiffness in her spine gradually lessen as their voices faded on the stairs. It was odd that Prudence Carroll had that effect on her . . . making her as prickly as a porcupine. It had always been the same — even before she learned of the friendship that had leaped to life between the film star and Rennie Bruce.

She knew that her respect for Bart's judgement should have prompted her into some degree of liking for the woman who was his most constant companion. Bart ran round in circles to please her . . . and he was not a man to give so much of himself unless he loved, Georgina thought drily. It was commonly believed that they would marry eventually despite the gossip that linked his name with other women and made much of any fleeting flirtation that Prudence enjoyed with another man. It seemed that Bart felt that Prudence Carroll had more to offer him than any of those other women in his life. And Prudence had told the world on numerous occasions through the media of press and television that Bart was the man she wanted to marry. He did not seem to mind the public flaunting of his private affairs but he did not confirm or deny the existence of an engagement. Challenged, he would merely smile, shrug and murmur a careless comment on the uncertainty of life with all its many corners still to be rounded.

Privately, Georgina did not think that Bart Blair would ever marry at all. He was thirty-five and dedicated to bachelorhood and the *Elysium* meant far more to him than any woman, she felt. It might seem to be just another theatre to anyone who did not understand his involvement with it . . . in fact, it was Bart's very reason for living and Georgina was convinced that he loved it more than he would ever love a mere woman. The *Elysium* had been founded by his great-great-grandfather and kept alive by a succession of devoted and stubborn Blairs who would not admit defeat even when creditors were pounding on the very doors of the theatre. Somehow, the shabby little theatre had survived every crisis . . . and under Bart's skilful and intuitive direction it had become a thriving and much respected concern.

There was certainly some kind of magic about the theatre that seemed to cast a spell on everyone associated with it. Georgina had known a strange sense of nostalgia that puzzled her for some time until she learned that it was the *Elysium* where her parents had once appeared together and she had been taken as a small child to see them on stage for the first time. The beautiful, resonant voice of her famous father and the vitality and warmth of her lovely mother, perfect foil and superb complement, had seemed to captivate the entire audience. The occasion had left a lasting impression on Georgina's young mind and probably planted the first seed of her love for the theatre and her own desire to be involved with it in some way.

She was very happy at the *Elysium* which seemed to hold all the magic of those memorable days before her father died so tragically and her mother retired from the theatre to write novels. The theatre had always played a great part in her life and the *Elysium* seemed to crystallise all that she had ever felt for the magic world of drama and she wholly understood why her predecessor had struggled to work when she was so ill and still could not relinquish all her involvement despite her failing health. For Evelyn Pritchard came in every day to release Georgina for a few hours . . . a system that worked well and suited everyone admirably.

The elderly Evelyn had originally suggested that Bart should ask the clever young Georgina Durrell to take over the real burden of secretarial work while she continued on a part-time basis as long as her health allowed. She had pointed out that the working day would seem very long to a modern girl, ten in the morning until eight at night, and that it might be a good idea to arrange matters so that Georgina worked until two, when Evelyn would take over, and returned again at five. The free afternoon would compensate her for the late evenings.

And Georgina certainly found it very convenient to be free each afternoon to shop, to clean her tiny flat, to enjoy the sunshine on a lovely day, to meet her friends, to visit the hairdresser or dentist or simply to laze with a book or some music. And she loved the hustle and bustle of the early evening when the theatre hummed in readiness for the performance and she might be called upon for a variety of tasks. It was a demanding job but an exciting one and she enjoyed every minute of it . . .

3

GEORGINA always had a lot to do and there were always interruptions and that morning was no exception. The telephone shrilled frequently. People dropped in for advice or instructions or a friendly gossip or merely in the hope of getting to Bart through his secretary and she managed to find time for them all while coping with everything else.

Yet her thoughts were strangely haunted by the warm and loving smile that Bart had bestowed on Prudence earlier . . . it seemed to hover in her mind's eye like the grin of the Cheshire Cat in *Alice* and she was puzzled by the vague feeling of hurt that accompanied the recollection.

He should smile more often in just that particular way, she decided. He was a most attractive man yet he could

41

look quite grim on occasions. The intense dedication that he brought to his work often meant that he forgot to smile and could be brusque and quick-tempered and even harsh. Most people stood in awe of him and some feared the caustic tongue and others dreaded the smallest sign of his disapproval. Georgina had supposed him to be the cold and forbidding tyrant that he seemed until she knew him better and realised that for all his bark he was a warm, kindly and very human person.

He seemed to reserve the full impact of his charm for the women in his life and, as a mere secretary, Georgina did not come into that category. She knew that he liked her well enough and appreciated her efficiency but he kept her at a distance and she was content to be just a piece of office equipment to him.

That experience with Rennie had left its mark and she did not want to become deeply involved with any man. For that reason, she chose her men-friends very carefully. Stuart, for instance, was very safe for while he fancied himself in love with her she knew that it would not suit him at all if she took him seriously. Unrequited love was the spur he needed to write and she was merely the latest in a long line. Lucas was safe, too . . . very much the man about town, the carefree bachelor, he was only interested in light affairs. And Paul who had loved her faithfully for some years and was her dear friend and accepted that he could never be anything more. And there were other men who were simply friends with never the slightest suggestion of romance to spoil things. It was just the way that Georgina wanted it . . .

Bart came back to the theatre just before two o'clock, as promised, and brought Evelyn with him, having detoured on his way back from the airport to save her the journey from Victoria.

Evelyn Pritchard was a tiny woman

with neat, iron-grey hair and a sweet expression and she was a well known and much-loved personality in London's theatreland. It had taken some time for Georgina to impress her own identity on various associates and agencies and actors who had been used to linking Evelyn Pritchard with the *Elysium* and Blair Productions for so many years.

She was a gentle, kindly person and Georgina had quickly become fond of her and had much cause to be grateful to her above and beyond the unknown fact that she owed her job to Evelyn's recommendation. She was growing old and looking frail but she refused to retire and everyone knew that the *Elysium* was the kingpin of her existence. Georgina was considerate and tactful, always contriving to leave some unfinished work for Evelyn's attention which would not make too many demands on her and yet confirmed her belief that she was still needed. Certainly she was invaluable for knowing the right contacts and just how to approach them, for smoothing out problems among the theatre staff and for bridging the gap when members of the cast quarrelled . . . a not infrequent occurrence with so much temperament flying about the theatre at times!

Georgina admired her very much and set out to learn all she could from the frail little woman with so much experience of the theatre . . . and wondered if in time to come she would be a similar figure in theatreland, an elderly spinster with all the knowledge at her fingertips, the affection and respect of the famous and the virtually unknown — and scarcely any personal life outside the theatre. Evelyn had many memories of the past but they all seemed to be linked with the *Elysium* and the Blairs, past productions, stars she had known and loved. No husband, no children, no home of her own for she had always lived with a married sister, it was scarcely surprising that she looked upon the theatre as her home and loved Bart as dearly as if he were her son, Georgina thought.

For all her bitterness, her resolution to avoid loving and the pain it brought, Georgina did not want to end her days as a lonely old woman who went on working because it was her only reason for living. She was young and the blood flowed softly in her veins and old age was a lifetime away . . . but sometimes she looked at Evelyn and fancied that she saw herself in the distant future and felt alarm for there was a strong instinct within her for marriage and motherhood. Perhaps too strong an instinct for it had surely been that too-eager grasping at the promise of such things that had lost her the man she loved. If she had been wiser, more patient, she and Rennie might still be together, she often mourned, remembering only that she had loved too intensely and forgetting that he had never loved at all . . .

With Evelyn's arrival, she was free for the afternoon and it had turned into a beautiful day with no trace of the morning's rain. But Georgina went out into the bright sunshine with a strange heaviness of heart . . . and Evelyn looked at her thoughtfully.

"Something on that child's mind," she said quietly, a little troubled. She had grown fond of Georgina and felt that the girl's sunny nature brought a new brightness and a new warmth to the office.

Bart laughed indulgently. "You just need to worry about someone," he teased her gently. "It used to be me but as I haven't given you an ounce of trouble in years you've found a substitute in Georgina. What do you imagine is wrong?"

"She isn't happy," Evelyn said with a firmness that dismissed the implication that it was imagination.

Bart frowned, finding it vaguely disturbing to associate Georgina with unhappiness for she was young and pretty and wholesome and deserved better . . . even if she was a shocking flirt! He brushed aside the unease. "Oh, women enjoy being a little unhappy, don't they? The high and the lows of emotion apparently make life more interesting for them," he said cynically. "But I think you are mistaken, Evelyn . . . I doubt if she has anything on her mind other than the new boy-friend!"

She looked interested. "Is there a new boy-friend?" She was too shrewd to be deceived by the seeming flirtatiousness that appeared to annoy Bart much more than it should considering that he was merely the girl's employer. She suspected that Georgina's fickle behaviour was a cover for heartache . . . and she also suspected that Bart liked the girl much more than he was prepared to admit even to himself. A man like Bart Blair would not readily welcome the thought that a woman could be more important to him than his work, she thought, a little ruefully.

"*I* don't know!" Bart exclaimed impatiently. "She doesn't confide in me! But she was dancing the night away with Lucas Winfull and seemed to be enjoying it!"

"Oh, well . . . young people shouldn't always be thinking about serious things," Evelyn said indulgently.

Bart smiled wryly. It was obvious that she meant to approve of her youthful successor come what may . . . for some reason, Georgina had been the apple of her eye from the beginning. Bart wondered if Evelyn had cherished a secret affection for the girl's father . . . certainly he had been one of the matinée idols who figured so largely in her reminiscences. Perhaps her affection and approval were tinged with memories of her own youth when, if she were to be believed, she had been even more of a flirt than Georgina and captivated the hearts of some of the most famous names in the theatre. Yet she had apparently remained heartwhole for she had never married and, according to her own account, never regretted her single state.

But Bart did wonder if she had chanced to love the unattainable . . . such as Richard Durrell, for instance.

"I believe you encourage her," he said in mock reproach. "I've heard you recounting your lurid past and I'm sure you must have told her that there's safety in numbers!"

Evelyn chuckled. "So there is! But she doesn't need my advice, Bart . . . she can take good care of herself! She's much too sensible to get involved in a permanent relationship too soon. She won't make the mistake of plunging into marriage before she knows anything about men."

Bart raised an amused eyebrow. "I expect she knew all about men in her cradle, my dear Evelyn," he said drily, took a couple of scripts from the pile waiting to be read and went into his office with an air of having wasted far too much time on the trivial . . .

Georgina walked homewards, a slender, pretty girl in a vivid summer dress that caught the eye, the sun touching her soft hair to gold, her step lacking a little of its usual bounce and her smile lacking a little of its usual vivacity as she nodded to people she knew.

She wished she could account for the odd depression which had suddenly descended. It had been a hectic morning but she had learned to take that in her stride and she enjoyed it all too much to believe it could be to blame for her low spirits. She was not at all tired and she was already looking forward to the evening. It was not unusual for her to remain at the theatre all day if she had no definite plans, watching a rehearsal or helping out in the wardrobe or merely enjoying the company and conversation of anyone who was briefly idle.

She had been anxious about the future of *Devil's Delight*, more for the sake of Stuart's feelings than because she had any personal stake in the play's future. But it had been reprieved so there was no cause for depression in that direction. Surely she was not piqued because Stuart had been so swiftly taken with Prudence Carroll's charms? She was fond of Stuart but there was no romantic involvement on her part. He was a good friend but nothing more . . . and yet, if one was being honest, perhaps it had hurt a little that she had been virtually pushed aside as soon as Prudence appeared on the scene. And if one was being honest . . . well, she could not help feeling a little envious of the woman who had so much. So many fairy godmothers had showered gifts at her christening, it seemed . . . beauty, charm, self-possession, talent and the gift of winning hearts with a mere smile.

Smile . . . ! That was it! The realisation hit her like a blow in the stomach. For some reason, she was still haunted by the loving smile that Bart had bestowed on Prudence as they went from the office. The look in his eyes had twisted Georgina's foolish heart into jealous knots. Oh, not that she wanted him to smile on her so warmly . . . she was not jealous of *his* feelings for Prudence! She merely felt that Prudence should be content with the love of a man like Bart and not encourage the attentions of other men . . . particularly Rennie Bruce!

It had twisted the knife in the wound to see so much love, so much tenderness, openly betrayed by Bart when her own heart ached so painfully for a man who had never looked at her in just that way. She clung to the belief that Rennie had loved her a little but it was heart-breakingly obvious that Bart loved Prudence very, very much. It was equally obvious that she did not love him enough to discourage other men from paying court to her . . . Bart was surely destined to be badly hurt, Georgina thought unhappily. Just as she had been hurt and was still being hurt. Time was supposed to be the great healer, she thought with bitterness. Well, it was a year since she had kissed goodbye to all her hopes where Rennie was concerned and the pain could still catch her when she least expected it and she was as much in love with him as ever!

She really had begun to believe that she might be getting over him at last. She had dined and danced with Lucas on the previous evening and enjoyed the warm flattering in his attentions, finding a feminine delight in the knowledge that he found her attractive. Her heart had lifted a little at the touch of his lips and her body had melted a little in his embrace, later that evening. But suddenly it had not been Lucas who held her . . . suddenly he had seemed to smile with Rennie's smile and look at her with Rennie's eyes and her heart had plunged with despair because it should have been Rennie who held her and wanted her and hinted at loving her. Abruptly she had pulled away from the strong arms that reminded her too much of the urgent embrace she had once known.

Lucas had accepted her withdrawal without comment but she knew that she had hurt him . . . and it had been impossible for her to explain. How could she expect any man to understand her continued obsession with the past, of her fear that the swift tide of passion, so easily aroused in her, might sweep her irrevocably towards greater regret.

She had watched the tail lights of his car vanish in the distance and wondered how much longer their friendship would last. For no man liked rebuff. It was foolish to allow Rennie to ruin every promising relationship that chance threw in her way. Yet it happened time and again, she thought bitterly as she let herself into the dark, lonely flat. Rennie would intrude at the most inconvenient of moments. The intolerable ache could begin again without warning and instead of finding balm for her heartache and humiliation with another man she seemed destined to hand out heartache and humiliation in her turn!

The intensity of her feeling for Rennie and the treatment she had received at his hands must always colour her attitude to other men, it seemed. For she was convinced that she could never again give her heart so trustingly . . . and certainly she would never again give herself to any man unless she could be absolutely sure that he truly loved her and would not treat her as Rennie had. Loving as she had loved Rennie had given him far too much power over her emotions and her peace of mind, she thought ruefully. The kind of love he had inspired had created a force that could still affect her life all these lonely and despairing months later.

Despite everything, she loved him still . . . and she was abruptly filled with longing for him. She ached for his arms about her, the magic in his kiss, the delight in his whispered endearments — and she ached most of all for the lost confidence in herself and her ability to win a man's love and hold it always . . .

Thinking of Rennie with such intensity, she turned swiftly at the sound of her name as though very desire must have conjured his appearance. But the tall man who had hailed her was not the man she still loved so foolishly. She had not seen her cousin Mathew for some months and pleasure leaped immediately to her smile as he hurried towards her.

He swept her into his arms and kissed her soundly in full view of the amused public. "Hallo, Gorgeous!" he greeted her extravagantly. He drew away to smile at her with undisguised admiration and affection. "You know, of all my cousins, you are undeniably the prettiest, Georgie!" he declared warmly.

She laughed up at him. As his only girl cousin, she could accept the truth of the compliment without conceit! "You *are* an idiot," she said affectionately.

"But what are you doing here?" she demanded, tucking her hand in his arm and drawing him towards the mansions where she lived.

"Passing through, more or less . . . I'm flying to Cape Town on Friday", he said lightly. "I tried to telephone from the station and then remembered that you were at work. I couldn't recall the name of the theatre but I knew that you were home about two. How are you, Georgie . . . fighting fit? I shall want you to help me paint the town red in the next few days, you know!"

Georgina felt a warm glow of affection for him. He was not only a dear and a great friend since childhood. He had turned up just in time to rescue her from a bout of self-pity and she was grateful. She smiled at him a little emotionally.

"It *is* good to see you," she said emphatically. "Where are you staying? I can put you up, you know . . . if you don't object to the sofa?"

"Not that lumpy old thing I slept

on last time, Georgie?" he demanded in mock horror.

She giggled. "It is lumpy," she admitted honestly. "I wish I were generous enough to offer my bed but I'm afraid you'd take it! Can you bear the sofa? I do want you to stay," she said coaxingly. "It's such an age since you were last in town and we must have a million things to tell each other!"

He smiled down at her. "You make me an offer I can't refuse," he assured her warmly. He followed her through the archway into the open court of the mansions and looked about him at the shabby buildings, monument to Victorian architecture. "This place doesn't change much, does it . . . except to get grimier."

"It's home," Georgina returned lightly, almost affectionately. "Convenient, cheap and really quite comfortable. A lot of people envy me my flat right in the heart of theatreland. And it is a cosy little place, after all . . . "

4

"COSY is the word," Mathew echoed wryly, his broad height seeming to dwarf the tiny kitchen with its bright paint and gay curtains and gleaming equipment.

"Eaten lately?" Georgina asked, putting on the kettle.

"Oh, I had something on the train . . . "

"Ham and salad, coffee, cheese and biscuits," she suggested, already at work on preparations for the meal.

He nodded. "Great!" He watched her for a few moments, smiling. Then he said lightly: "You'd be a wonderful wife, Georgie . . . you have all the right qualities."

She turned a laughing face to him. "I take it that *isn't* a proposal?"

"Lord, no . . . unbiased comment," he assured her, pretending alarm.

60

"Don't be anxious," she said with a smile that suddenly did not reach her eyes. "I'm not looking for a husband. In fact, I'm off marriage . . . it isn't fashionable just now."

He studied her thoughtfully. Then he said gently: "Still raw, Georgie?"

She was about to deny that she had ever been hurt and then she remembered that this was Mathew who knew and understood all that had happened. "I'm a fool," she said stiffly. "It's a long time ago and it should have stopped hurting by now."

"But it hasn't . . . "

There was obvious compassion in his quiet tone. Georgina forced back the tears that suddenly threatened. "Oh, I always did take everything too seriously," she said, wondering how much she had actually told him about that affair with Rennie . . . she could vaguely remember that she had desperately needed a confidant and a shoulder to cry on and he had been there at a time when her pride had

61

abruptly deserted her. Later she had been thankful that it had been Mathew who was the soul of discretion.

There was a faintly rueful smile in his eyes as he looked down at her. "Except me," he said quietly.

Georgina was doubtful, not sure if he was teasing. One could never really trust his sense of humour. She decided not to pursue the matter. "What are you going to do in South Africa . . . more research?" she asked brightly. "Are you working on a new book? Or is it just a holiday?" Mathew was an anthropologist and the author of several successful books on the history of mankind. It always astonished her to connect her light-hearted, carefree cousin with such a heavyweight and responsible subject.

He shook his head. "I'm going to be married," he said, delighting in the astonishment that leaped to her pretty face. "I have old-fashioned tastes, you see."

"Married!" she echoed incredulously.

Then she laughed and shook her head. "I don't believe it!"

"It's the unlikeliest thing that ever happened to me," he agreed lightly. "I'm a bachelor by instinct."

"Then how . . . ? Oh, do be serious and explain yourself properly, Mathew!" she chided him.

He composed his features to seriousness but his eyes danced with mischief as he said: "I am going out to Cape Town to be married and I hope to be back next month with my wife." He smiled. "You shall meet her then, doubting Georgie!"

"Seeing will be believing!" she jeered. "But who is she? How did it happen? Tell me!" Like any woman, she was interested in the romantic affairs of other people. She simply did not want to become involved in romance herself for a very long time . . .

"Her name is Amanda. She's twenty-two and very attractive and much too good for me — and too stubborn to accept the fact. I didn't have a chance, of course. She took one look and made up her mind to marry me — and when you meet Amanda you'll discover that when she makes up her mind to something there's no way out!"

He spoke with a levity that belied the warm tenderness in his expression and Georgina felt her heart contract with that little spasm of jealousy. She was happy for Mathew . . . of course she was! He was obviously very much in love and looking forward to the marriage which must surprise everyone who knew his light-hearted outlook on love and life. But she seemed destined just now to meet with reminders of all the happy lovers that there were in the world — and how lonely and unhappy she continued to be without Rennie.

She pushed the thought of him from her mind and plied Mathew with eager questions about his Amanda . . . how and where they had met, when and where they were to be married, their plans for the future — and all the time was careful to conceal the heaviness of her own heart so that his delight should not be shadowed by her pain. It was no one's fault that she had fallen in love only to know heartache and humiliation . . . least of all Mathew's who would have given much to spare her the least hurt, she knew.

Mathew, deeply in love and wishing away the seeming eternity before he took flight for Cape Town and Amanda, could have happily spent hours describing how, when and where his life had changed so miraculously. But he was sensitive to the pain that still lurked in his cousin's heart and soon, without overdone tact, he turned the subject to family matters and mutual friends and her work at the theatre and plans for the few days he meant to spend in town.

Time flew in his company and much too soon Georgina had to return to work. She felt a momentary impatience with her job and then reminded herself that she was usually content with the odd hours and that there would be plenty of time to be with Mathew before he flew off to South Africa.

He walked to the theatre with her and then went off to look up some friends. Georgina looked after him, a smile of pure affection curving her lips, a warmth in her eyes that hinted at tenderness.

Bart, pushing through the swing doors of the theatre, paused to look at the luminously lovely face.

His eyes narrowed with a kind of impatient amusement. What an actress, he thought with reluctant admiration. Only the night before he had been almost convinced that Lucas Winfull was the only man who mattered to her — and no doubt Lucas had also been deceived. Now she conveyed the impression that the departing man was the dearest thing in life to her. She could not be in love with all the men in her life, Bart thought drily . . . she was merely a past-mistress at the art of flirtation.

He turned away with a flicker of contempt. Her main interest in life seemed to be the unceasing acquisition of admirers . . . and he had no time for the kind of woman who used men to inflate her ego and to enjoy the good life. Certainly any man who believed the lie in her shining eyes or the coquetry in her sweet smile or the promise in her soft voice must be a fool beyond redemption, he thought with a harshness that he believed to be justified.

Evelyn pleaded the girl's youth, the generous nature, the warm heart that swept her so light-heartedly from one man to another but Bart could not feel that there was any excuse for a woman who encouraged men to care for her only to discard them as soon as she grew bored. Having seen her in action, Bart did not believe that it was all unconscious encouragement on her part. It seemed to him that she deliberately set out to win a man's love because it gratified her vanity and that she then callously ignored the pain that she inflicted by her refusal or inability to love in return. He had seen her with too many men. He was experienced enough to recognise the signs by which a man betrayed himself when in love and he knew that men found it easy to love his pretty secretary. He did not deny her appeal for most men. But he viewed her dispassionately and felt that she was not to be trusted with any man's heart . . . she was fickle, selfish and egotistical. Collecting hearts was her hobby and he scarcely knew whether he despised most the heartless Georgina or the fools who fell for her captivating prettiness and appealing femininity . . .

Prudence showered to refresh herself after the flight, donned a loose, flowing gown and went out to the balcony that overlooked the sea. It was a very attractive villa that the film company had rented for her use with its private beach and extensive grounds together with a very efficient staff.

She sipped a long, cool drink and watched the waves lapping on the shore and thought about Bart with the comforting knowledge that she could not be very far from his thoughts. Dear, reliable Bart . . .

There had been a certain promise in his kiss when they parted at the airport. There had also been an unusual degree of possessiveness in his manner which might well have been meant for Rennie's observation, she thought shrewdly. She was sure that her friendship with Rennie Bruce troubled Bart whereas he had shown a smiling unconcern in response to her interest in all other men in the past. Perhaps he was seriously thinking of marriage at last, she thought hopefully.

She had never wished to rush Bart into anything but her patience ought to have its reward. A man's ambition and dedication were very important to him, she admitted, but they were bleak companions for one's old age. Bart was far from old but he was at the age when a man should marry if he did not mean to remain a bachelor all his life, Prudence felt. She was quite sure that even the most dedicated bachelor reached a point in time when marriage held a certain appeal . . . and she meant to be around when Bart reached that point!

She had made up her mind to marry him when they first met and there had never been any man to compare with him since that day. She had never allowed him to monopolise her, of course . . . it was bad for any man to know that he was the one and only in a woman's life! Bart knew that she cared for him but there were many degrees of loving and she had never allowed him to assume that she would marry him if he proposed it. She believed that he loved her but she could not be one hundred per cent certain and there were other women in his life and so it had put new hope into her heart to see the glowing warmth in his eyes and sense the new tenderness in his kiss.

It was annoying that she had left London at a time when a little strategy might have won her what she wanted. But she hoped that Bart would manage a few days away from the theatre . . . and the romantic Riviera might bring about the one thing that all the months in practical England had failed to achieve!

She was impatient to start shooting the new film although she was a little anxious if she would do justice to the demanding part. Yet she knew quite instinctively that the part might have been written for her and that the film would be a fantastic success now that it was finally off the ground after long weeks of discussion and argument. She was a little nervous of working with a new director of whom she knew nothing except that he was reputed to be brilliant . . . and very demanding.

Meeting him on the set the following day, Prudence was disconcerted by the brusque manner of the man. She was to play a very big part in the film and she was a successful and internationally-known star yet John Jordan took no notice of her and scarcely spoke to her. She was taken aback and faintly angry and convinced that she ought to dislike him on principle. But she found herself excusing him as a busy, dedicated man who did not have time to spare for the trivia of social convention. Moreover, she found that she was fascinated by the man with his compelling personality and physical magnetism.

She arrived punctually on set after attending wardrobe and make-up and found everyone involved in technical problems. Three hours and a succession of irritations later, she was finally called to work on the first scenes.

Jordan was looking grim and he wasted no time at all on pleasantries. He told Prudence what he wanted of her in the tone of voice that implied his determination to get it at all costs. He was a burly man with a mass of black hair that grew in tight curls at the nape of his neck. He had the lean good looks of the sensitive Jew and his penetrating eyes were a brilliant and very beautiful blue. He had a forceful personality, a great deal of dynamic energy and an attitude that implied that the cast were merely puppets that must move and speak at his bidding.

It was a long day on the set beneath the hot sun. Prudence was a very gifted actress . . . more important to a man like Jordan, she was willing to be directed and possessed a quick understanding and knew instinctively what he required. He relaxed as shooting continued with comparatively few hitches and he found that Prudence Carroll was as easy to direct and as delightful to work with as he had been assured.

Prudence blossomed beneath his approval and set herself to delight and astonish him, scarcely knowing why it should matter so much that he should be pleased with her efforts. Some kind of rapport was swiftly established between them and at moments during the long day everything else faded to insignificance on the crowded set . . . only Jordan and his sensitive, clever direction and her own intuitive response existed for them both.

The day was too long and people began to grumble, to grow restless, to make foolish mistakes . . . excepting Prudence who responded with new delight and new depth to the warm encouragement in the director's approving smile. He stimulated her and banished all awareness of weariness and she would happily have worked throughout the night if he had demanded it. But the sun began to set and even the inexhaustible Jordan was forced to call a halt to shooting.

Prudence relaxed in the luxurious caravan that did double duty as dressing-room and sitting-room, knowing that she was absolutely exhausted. But she was also oddly happy. It had been a memorable day . . . a day she would never forget!

She had sent her dresser away and she was alone, waiting, excitement and elation and just a little trepidation battling within her for supremacy. Her heart began to pound in her throat and the colour stormed into her lovely face at the sound of a man's step and a low knock on the caravan door. He had come just as she had known that he must! He knew just as she did that something had sparked between them that day . . . something too vital, too real to be ignored!

A little breathless, she called: "Come . . . !" She rose eagerly to welcome him, past caring for the pretence of convention, and held out both hands with the impulsive confidence in his response to the swift enchantment in her own blood.

Jordan took her hands and looked down at her, unsmiling. She was alone, as he had expected. She wore a flowing white robe and her beautiful hair was loose on her shoulders. She was slightly flushed and the quick rise and fall of her breast betrayed the inner excitement.

She looked up at him with wide, expectant eyes. Jordan had met this reaction to his physical magnetism in many women and it usually left him quite cold and wholly indifferent. He knew that he was very attractive to women and it was something that he had learned to accept and only to use when it suited him. He suddenly discovered that he was not at all indifferent to this woman. She was very beautiful with the promise of all that a man might desire.

"I came to thank you," he said formally. "I've seen the first rushes and they are good . . . very good. It's an excellent beginning." Suddenly he smiled into the lovely eyes that were on a level with his own . . . for he was a small man and no Adonis for all his swift conquest of women.

Prudence trembled, suddenly, unexpectedly on fire for him. Ignoring the formal tone, the lack of response in the cool clasp of his hands, she seized on the reassurance in the smile that touched his very blue eyes. "The beginning of more than just a film," she said softly and with growing confidence.

Her heart soared. They would dine together and dance a little, she decided. Tired though she was, she wanted to be with him . . . with weariness etching itself in every muscle in her slender body, she knew she could dance all night in his arms. When they had dined and danced and talked and laughed together, they would love together, she thought, her pulses quickening with eager anticipation for he would surely be a wonderful lover . . . gentle, tender, yet demanding, sweeping her to unsuspected heights of ecstasy. She wanted him as she had never wanted any man . . .

Suddenly a little shy, she withdrew her hands and turned towards the sideboard with its array of bottles and decanters and glasses. "We must have a drink . . . drink a toast to the success of the film," she said gaily, deciding that he was as tense, as emotionally overstrung as she was . . . one did not meet one's destiny every day, after all!

"Not now, thanks . . . I still have a great deal of work to do tonight," he said carefully.

Prudence's heart contracted with disappointment. She turned swiftly. "Oh, don't go! I thought . . . I mean, I hoped we would . . . I wanted to ask you to have dinner with me." She was stumbling on the words like a gauche schoolgirl but suddenly all her confidence had deserted her.

He hesitated. "You are tired. It has been a long day."

She relinquished the last hold on her pride without regret. "Please . . . !"

Jordan stood very still, very tense, meeting the glowing green eyes with all their desperate appeal. She was very beautiful and she was offering herself with warm generosity. As she had given to his demands during the long and tiring day, so she would give herself to his arms with unhesitating surrender . . . the inevitable extension of the intimacy which had sparked to life between them.

Desire stirred strongly. He was a sensual man who had always taken what he wanted without regard for the consequences. But he hesitated, instinctively sensing a new and unsuspected danger in taking this woman. No woman had ever inspired him to love. He did not believe in the fantasy that others described as loving. But he hesitated, suddenly reluctant to claim the promised sweetness of her lips, the delights to be found in her embrace . . . such sweetness, such delight might become too important, too disturbing.

"I am sorry . . . I have people waiting for me," he said gently. He lifted one of the small, slender hands to his lips and kissed it and there was a very sober expression in the blue eyes that looked down at her lovely face.

In another moment, he had gone . . .

5

PRUDENCE marvelled that any man could be so blind, so deaf, so lacking in perception. He *must* have seen and heard and sensed the wanting that consumed her. She could not, would not, believe that he could be immune to the warm loveliness that stirred other men so swiftly. He must want her! Yet he had left her without any hint of that wanting, any promise for the morrow . . . left her to an agony of longing and a swift, strange fever in her blood. It was impossible to go after him, to throw herself into his arms, to beg for the ease of mind and heart and body that suddenly and strangely only he could provide.

She loved him completely and utterly . . . a man she had never met until that day. She did not know how or why it had happened. But the love that she had supposed she felt for Bart suddenly seemed a pale and feeble thing in comparison with this fierce and certain need for a man who was surely her destiny. This was loving such as she had never imagined or thought to know . . . and it was impossible that Jordan did not feel exactly as she did! So why, why, why had he left her so abruptly without the smallest comfort for the tumult and terror in her heart. For supposing he did not care and never cared! She would want to die, she thought bleakly and without drama, for there would be no point in life without him . . .

A sound sent her hurtling to open the door of the caravan and she almost tumbled into Jordan's arms before she realised that he was too tall, too broad, too young to be the director recalled by the cry of her heart.

Rennie Bruce steadied her with both hands on the slender waist. "Now that's what I call a welcome," he said, smiling.

He was extremely good-looking and very blond, a smooth, suave, sure of himself young man — and just now he was very sure that Prudence was about to yield to his subtle persuasions. For some weeks she had responded to his light and skilful attentions with encouraging friendliness and she was obviously attracted to him . . . and he was confident that the coming weeks with their promised proximity would bring a new intimacy to their relationship.

Prudence forced a smile. "Sorry . . . I lost my balance," she said lightly disengaging herself from his embrace. "What can I do for you, Rennie?"

He grinned, a little mischievously. "That's a leading question, my sweet."

Prudence was too tired and dispirited to respond to the flirtatious approach. Suddenly he seemed very young and unexciting and she marvelled that she had found him attractive or interesting in the past weeks. She wondered if she would always compare a man with the challenge that was Jordan now that she had met and recognised her destiny . . . and knew the answer. Jordan was very much a man and Rennie seemed an inexperienced boy in comparison despite his reputation for liking women a little too well.

"Darling, I'm tired," she said with faint impatience. "Help yourself to a drink if you want and then perhaps you'd like to take me home."

He moved to the decanters and poured whisky into a glass. He looked over his shoulder at her, a faint frown in his eyes. "I thought we were going to the Casino."

"Oh, not tonight, Rennie . . . I don't think I can face it after all." She smiled at him with a warmth that meant to lessen disappointment but only encouraged him in the conviction that she was near to surrender. He swiftly discarded the idea of the Casino. It might be much more to his advantage to spend the evening at the villa . . . an intimate dinner by candlelight and drinks on the moonlit terrace and his own particular brand of persuasion might be a combination she could not resist . . .

Prudence was abstracted, scarcely listening when he spoke, sipping absently at a drink, allowing a cigarette to burn neglected between her fingers. Rennie leaned against the stone balustrade, studying her thoughtfully, wondering where he was failing and why she was so preoccupied. She was probably tired. Jordan was a brute of a director and had almost worked her into the ground. He turned away to stare down at the shore and the lapping waves. The setting was very romantic but he was simply not getting any co-operation, he thought wryly. The slightest overture had met with rebuff. He was just not existing for her that night, he thought ruefully.

He reached out a hand to stroke her soft cheek, gently. She turned her beautiful face to him and smiled . . . but the smile did not reach her eyes.

"I'm poor company," she said without regret. He had virtually invited himself to dinner and she had felt too apathetic to send him away. But now he was an irritation. He talked, he demanded her attention, he obviously desired to make love to her — and all she wanted was to be left alone with her thoughts of Jordan and the topsy-turvy tumbling of her emotions.

"You are exhausted," he said, a little angrily. "I'm amazed that anyone could be so insensitive . . . Jordan must have known that he was too demanding. I'm astonished that you allowed it, Prudence!"

She shrugged, understanding the reason for his annoyance and quite indifferent to his disappointment. She had become fond of him in recent weeks and perhaps she might have been tempted to yield to his undeniable attraction for her . . . if Jordan had not suddenly entered her life to turn it upside-down and make himself the only man in all the world that she could ever want. Now she could not even bear the thought of Rennie's lips on her own or his arms about her in close embrace and she regretted the amount of encouragement that she had given him of late.

"He's a stimulating director," she said carelessly. "On the set I didn't feel at all tired or overworked. But now . . . darling, I'm going to send you away and tumble into bed. Do you mind?" She was not so much tired as bored and irritated — and she marvelled at his lack of perception.

There was nothing that Rennie could say or do in the face of such an obvious desire for him to go. So, forcing back chagrin, he slipped his arm about her and dropped a light kiss on her hair and left with as much grace as he could muster.

Prudence remained on the low balcony, her hair lifting in the soft breeze and a faraway look in her eyes . . . and below her on the beach strolled the very man who occupied her thoughts.

Jordan found it relaxing to walk a little last thing at night . . . particularly at the end of a long and difficult day. So much talk, so many problems — he had doubted if shooting would ever begin on the new film. That very morning he had been close to washing his hands of the entire business . . . and then Prudence Carroll had walked on to the set and brought new hope, new incentive, new ambition to his dream. She was not just a brilliant actress playing a part of the woman who loved Bartok . . . she *was* the woman who loved Bartok, living and breathing and utterly convincing.

But off the set she was again the beautiful and very desirable woman who was too much on his mind as he walked along the shore that night. He did not know what caused him to look towards the villa as he passed. Perhaps it was the paleness of her gown in the moonlight that caught his eye . . . or the sudden movement that betrayed delight. Or perhaps it was the swift intake of her breath that carried to him in the still evening air and quickened him to sudden desire. He looked and saw her and halted and knew that she had been watching and waiting for him even though she had not known that he would walk that way or possibly even realised that they were neighbours. And in that moment he knew that the instinct within him had brought him to her villa all unconsciously.

He went towards her . . . and she leaned over the edge of the balcony to smile with warm delight and stretch out her hand to him.

"Jordan . . . " she said softly.

He took the slim hand and looked into her eyes for a long moment. Then he said firmly: "I'm coming up . . . " And he climbed up and over the stone balustrade with the agility of a boy.

Prudence went into his arms with a little sigh of thankfulness . . . and Jordan held her very close, his lips against her hair and a very sober light in his eyes. For he knew deep within himself that if he committed himself in any way to this woman it would be for ever. No other woman had ever stirred him as she did. This was his woman, he realised abruptly — and all other women in the world must fade to mere shadows in the light of her loveliness.

He drew away to look down at her, a little smile just dawning in his eyes. "This is not very conventional."

She put her hand against his cheek in a loving gesture, a tenderness. "We aren't conventional people, surely." She kissed him . . . a light kiss, a mere brushing of butterfly wings, against his lips.

His body was suddenly taut. "Take care," he said with urgency. "I'm not playing games!"

Prudence put her arms about him and nestled close. "Nor am I . . . I've never been more serious in my life," she said quietly, steadily.

He lifted her face with strong fingers

beneath the round chin. "You belie your name, my dear. It isn't prudence to give so much so soon to a man you scarcely know," he warned for it was essential that she realise the demands he would make on her if she once gave herself into his keeping.

She looked into his blue eyes and felt a quiet flow of happiness about her heart. "I know all I need to know," she said with simple sincerity. "I know you are a man to love . . . and I love you."

Her heart soared as he brought his mouth down on her own with a fierce and yet wholly tender passion that stirred a swift flow of desire in her blood. She surrendered heart and soul and body to his kiss . . . and it did not seem strange to either of them that they had never met before that day and yet would belong together for eternity . . .

It was a hectic week for Georgina. Mathew was set on a last fling and, failing Amanda, felt that his cousin

Georgie was the ideal companion for a man determined to enjoy all the sights and sounds of the great metropolis. Georgina could not and did not want to refuse his desire for her company at every possible moment. He was great fun and she was glad of his company and affection. He had lifted her out of the doldrums and she could smile even when Bart was at his most difficult — and he was *very* difficult that week!

Distant yet demanding, icily cold and yet quick-tempered, more disapproving than ever, thought poor Georgina, discovering with a little shock of dismay that her employer regarded her with active dislike. She wondered at the sudden change in his attitude towards her. He had always been pleasant, courteous, even friendly . . . now he virtually snubbed the least pleasantry on her part, treated her with brusqueness bordering on rudeness and almost froze her to death with his cold disapproval. Georgina disliked working in such an atmosphere and she was beginning to wonder if she ought to leave the *Elysium*. But she had to make allowances for Bart. She supposed he must be missing Prudence . . . and, even more, he must be disturbed by the newspaper gossip about her tempestuous affair with the American film director. Something had sparked and burst into full flame apparently. Every day there was another story or yet another photograph depicting them together and 'very much in love' and admitting to their delight in each other. So far there was no mention of marriage or even an engagement but they were together day and night according to the press reports.

Georgina did not dare to mention the gossip to Bart but he was obviously aware of it and no one could doubt that he was deeply troubled by it and very hurt by Prudence's open disloyalty. After all, they were virtually engaged . . . or so Prudence had always encouraged everyone to believe! It was scarcely surprising that Bart had been in a foul mood ever since the story broke in the English press, Georgina thought wryly. He was the type who would be torn asunder by wild horses rather than admit his feelings to her or anyone else. She could only guess at the way he felt and make allowances for him and be his whipping-boy without complaint for a little while. After all, he was only human and he needed to vent his feelings on someone . . . and she was conveniently at hand.

He had some justification for finding fault with her that week, she admitted. Her mind was too often with Mathew and the day's plans or recalling the pleasure of the previous evening. She was not getting to bed until the early hours and despite her youth and resilience the pace inevitably was beginning to tell on her. She slipped away from the theatre earlier than she ought and came in later than she should . . . the days so hectic that she could scarcely find time for her job at all and would have asked for a holiday if it had not been such a busy week for Bart and everyone else.

For he and Stuart were looking at the play from a different slant, discussing ways and means of altering it sufficiently to please the public taste without losing any of its impact. Some lines had been deleted, others inserted and one scene had been completely re-written. The company had needed to learn and rehearse new lines and new 'business' at short notice and it had been a week of tension and irritations — a week when Bart would have appreciated the absolute peak of efficiency from his secretary, Georgina told herself ruefully, ripping yet another spoiled sheet from her typewriter and crumpling it.

She had a sheaf of notes to type for members of the cast . . . Bart's sometimes scathing comments, sometimes gently persuasive suggestions, which followed that afternoon's rehearsal and which he had dictated on Georgina's return from a lengthy luncheon given by friends to celebrate Mathew's forthcoming marriage. Too much food and wine at the wrong time of the day had given her a headache and she found it almost impossible to concentrate. Only her real affection for the *Elysium* and her job had brought her to the theatre that evening and the disapproval in Bart's expression as she entered the office, ten minutes late and elated by champagne, had almost sent her back to the party that she had reluctantly left.

Bart did not look up as she tossed the crumpled paper into the waste basket but a faint frown creased his brow. He was angry with Georgina, feeling that she had let him down badly all that week when she knew that he had much on his mind and particularly needed her efficient help. She was much too involved with her personal affairs at the moment and quite unable to give her full attention to her work. It seemed that everything must revolve around the new man in her life . . . including the *Elysium*!

The girl must be in love again, he thought impatiently — and wished she had chosen any week but this one to plunge into a new affair. She rushed from the theatre with mistakable eagerness, appeared to spend all her free time with the demanding Mathew, came reluctantly to the office to give only part of her mind to the day's work and never seemed to be there when he wanted her most! He was very disappointed. She had always seemed such a good girl, so willing and dependable and conscientious . . . and he had believed that she really cared about the theatre and its concerns.

One did not own the girl because one paid her an excellent salary, of course . . . but he did expect a certain loyalty and particularly at times of crisis! But she was just like every other woman, he thought a trifle bitterly . . . selfish and vain and concerned only with her own desires, ready to forsake all the old-fashioned virtues of loyalty and obligation the moment an attractive man loomed on the horizon!

There were shadows beneath her eyes and she looked pale, a little tense. Bart suspected that she was burning the candle at both ends. One moment she would be in high spirits, laughing and joking, elated and confident and obviously happy . . . the next moment she seemed to be serious, a little sad, inclined to introspection. Symptomatic of the disease called love, Bart decided drily. He did not suppose it was a very serious affair. He was inclined to think that Georgina fell in and out of love as though it was an amusing, delightful game without actually giving anything of herself to any man . . .

6

"IT doesn't seem to be my day," Georgina said ruefully, almost in defensive answer to the little frown that she sensed rather than saw. "I keep finding all the wrong keys."

"Then we must be thankful that you aren't playing the piano," he said sardonically.

Georgina's little gurgle of laughter brought a reluctant quirk of amusement to his own mouth. Encouraged, she said lightly, "Actually, I play the piano very well . . . I have a sensitive touch and a real feeling for music."

"Modesty, too," he commented drily.

Her eyes danced. "I'm quoting my music teacher," she said demurely.

"One day you must play something for me," he suggested smoothly. "We might be able to place you with the orchestra if your typing becomes too erratic."

She wrinkled her nose prettily, warmed by the unexpected smile in the words that was in such marked contrast to the unmistakable coldness of his manner during the week. Her heart lifted thankfully at the first signs of a thaw in the atmosphere.

"Ouch!" she said in laughing reproach. "That was below the belt!"

Meeting those dancing eyes and the warm sunshine in the lovely smile, Bart felt all the impact of her rich personality. In that moment, he knew why so many men found a golden enchantment in her smile and risked a great deal of heartache to know her better. In that moment he saw her for the first time despite all the months that he had known her . . . saw right through to the warm, appealing, wholly lovable nature that he had refused to believe could exist beneath the superficial flirtatiousness and lightness of manner.

There was no trace of coquetry in those laughing eyes or any hint of promise in that delightful smile . . . just a warm and generous outflowing of genuine friendliness that went straight to his heart in the most unexpected way and he smiled back at her with the rare, rich smile that he kept for his closest friends.

Georgina's heart gave a little jolt that was almost dismay. Knowing that he was so indifferent had given her a sense of security that she valued. She hastily dismissed the foolish fancy that there was something very remote from indifference in his smiling eyes. Feeling self-conscious, knowing that the colour had swept into her face, she reached for fresh paper and bent her head over the typewriter . . . and glanced up a moment or so later to discover that he was not paying her the slightest scrap of attention.

She was relieved. She did not want Bart to be even fleetingly attracted to her . . . some instinct within her being warned that there was safety in the impersonal relationship of employer-employee. As she left the theatre each evening she resolutely put him out of her mind and she did not expect or wish to remain in his thoughts. She had made a fool of herself over one man and she was resolved never to do so again and she was reluctant to become involved in any way with Bart Blair apart from her work. She simply accepted that he was the one man who might threaten her decision to have no more to do with the devil's delight that was loving . . .

Thankfully, she typed the last of the notes and tucked each one into its respective envelope. Then she rose from her desk to take them down to the notice board by the stage door that every member of the staff and company was supposed to check on arrival at the theatre.

Bart looked after her, a nerve throbbing in his lean jaw. It came as a shock to discover that he liked her very much more than he had known . . . much more than he truly wished, in fact. Perhaps he had been keeping her at a distance, quite unconsciously all these months, he thought wryly, instinctively aware of his vulnerability where she was concerned. He was astonished to discover that he was so vulnerable and that she had become incredibly important to him.

He had good reason to avoid becoming emotionally involved with Georgina Durrell, he reminded himself. For one thing, she had too many men paying court to her and he had no desire to swell the ranks. For another, he was not a marrying man and he rather suspected that loving a girl like Georgina would be synonymous with the desire to spend the rest of one's life with her . . . and that meant marriage!

He gave himself a mental shake. It was nonsense to suppose that he was anywhere near to loving Georgina! He had merely felt a brief, unimportant desire for her . . . a sudden, very natural response to her undeniable appeal. She was a lovely girl and the blood had quickened in his veins, warmed by her smile . . . but it was no more than a fleeting attraction, he told himself firmly. He would not give it another thought . . .

It was very obvious that she did not find him attractive, he decided wryly. She had never cast the smallest lure in his direction and a naturally flirtatious girl would not be deterred by the existence of another woman in his life, viz. Prudence who seemed to be rapidly moving out of his orbit if the newspaper stories were true! And a girl who could captivate any man she chose would not suppose him immune to her loveliness . . . so it followed that Georgina was indifferent to him as a man in his own right. He was merely her employer and no doubt she forgot him the moment she walked out of the office. Just as well, no doubt . . . and yet it might have been very pleasant to enjoy the company of someone like Georgina in his leisure hours.

He did not have the usual kind of affair with a pretty secretary in mind, of course. Georgina was not the girl to indulge in promiscuous affairs, he thought confidently . . . she might be a shocking flirt with a different boy-friend for every night of the week but he was quite convinced that she did not give herself lightly to any man. There was an air of touch-me-touch-me-not about Georgina which probably accounted for much of her appeal. But the biggest stumbling-block to his sudden and rather surprising desire to know more about her was obviously the man who currently filled her mind to the exclusion of almost everything else, he thought grimly.

She was an intelligent, level-headed girl as a rule. So she was either infatuated or very much in love at the moment. Bart had never known that kind of loving that dominated every thought and feeling and interfered with one's peace of mind and played havoc with one's life but he accepted that it could exist for a woman! He doubted that any man loved with that kind of dedication. *Man's love is of man's life a thing apart, 'tis woman's whole existence*, Byron had written — and Bart felt that the poet was probably right. Or had been in his day, he amended, remembering that women had become emancipated and were busily turning all the old traditions upside down! Love might be a weakness that a woman still found irresistible but he doubted if she still believed that happiness and peace of mind depended entirely on a smile of approval from the man she loved. But he felt that Georgina was an old-fashioned girl and her way of loving would be the old-fashioned way . . . her sudden changes of mood during that week seemed to prove that the man in her life was very much the axis on which her happiness revolved . . .

Time was passing and he was dreaming the minutes away, he realised abruptly. He rose, dismissing Georgina from his thoughts. There was time for a quick shower before he dressed for the evening.

His private quarters were very luxurious and very much a bachelor abode with its thick carpeting and deep leather furniture, its books and modern paintings, its expensive stereo equipment and well-equipped drinks cabinet. Very few people knew that the flat existed at the top of the theatre and only his intimates were invited within its walls for he preferred to do most of his entertaining at clubs and restaurants.

Even Georgina hesitated to intrude into that very private domain but the internal telephone was temporarily out of order and she needed to report a minor crisis backstage. She mounted the narrow stairway and knocked tentatively on the open door that led into a hallway with several doors leading off it. A moment later, she knocked again and called his name, rather shyly, entering the hallway. It was the first time that she had been to the flat, of course. But she was always very conscious that he jealously guarded his privacy . . . and just then she was particularly conscious that they were far from sight and sound of everyone else in the theatre. It was quite ridiculous and a terrible conceit to suppose that Bart Blair could have the slightest interest in her as a woman . . . but he was a man and she knew it was never wise to put the least temptation in a man's way! She knew from experience that the least likely of men could become amorous with the very smallest encouragement — or none at all!

Bart appeared in the open doorway of his bedroom, buttoning the dress shirt of palest blue with its frilled front. He smiled. "Is it an emergency?"

"Some of the lighting has failed," she said urgently. "Bryan is in a bit of a flap."

He nodded, quite unperturbed. "He'll cope," he said carelessly. "All the sooner for being left to get on with it. I've always found that extremity brings out the best in people."

Georgina looked at him doubtfully. It was unlike him to react so indifferently to anything that concerned the theatre. "And if he doesn't cope?"

He retreated into his bedroom to take his cuff-links from the dressing-table and fix them into his cuffs. "We need lights for the performance and Bryan will provide them," he said confidently, tossing the words over his shoulder. "Stage managers know how to work the necessary miracles when it's demanded."

She hesitated in the hallway. "Well, I've passed on the message," she said uncertainly. "I suppose Bryan will contact you himself if he needs advice."

"Undoubtedly — and I don't intend to rush backstage at the first hint of trouble. That would imply a lack of confidence in his ability, don't you think? Besides, we employ experienced technicians who should be able to put matters right," he reminded her, rather drily.

"Yes, of course," she agreed. "I expect Bryan merely thought you should be told . . . I interpreted it as a cry for help." She smiled. "I'm sorry I disturbed you," she added, turning away.

"Georgina . . . !"

She paused, suddenly wary without quite knowing or understanding why. "Yes . . . ?"

"Pour me a drink while I struggle with my tie . . . I think you know where things are kept." He smiled at her with friendly warmth. "You might like to join me . . . hair of the dog?" he suggested lightly.

She stiffened, a little indignant. Then she saw the friendliness in his eyes. "It was champagne," she admitted with a rueful smile. "Not the best drink for a working girl in the middle of the day!"

He raised his eyebrow. "Celebration?"

"My cousin's engagement," she said and did not elaborate because he could not be interested in her family affairs.

Bart nodded. "I see . . ." Not her own, anyway, he thought with relief. He was astonished to realise that it mattered that she had not rushed into an engagement with the man of the moment. He looked down at her, suddenly discovering how much he wanted her . . . the nearness of her and the soft perfume that emanated from her hair was playing havoc with his self-control. He turned away, almost abruptly . . .

When he entered the sitting-room, a few minutes later, Georgina handed him the brandy and soda that he liked. "Is it how you like it . . . not too much soda?" she asked, a little anxiously.

He tasted and then nodded. "Perfect — clever girl!" he said, smiling.

She grimaced. "Not always so clever," she said ruefully. "I seem to have done some very silly things this week!"

He shrugged. "We all have our off days."

She poured herself a small sherry. "I don't believe that you do," she said with the warmth of her admiration for him. "You never seem to make mistakes."

He laughed wryly. "I'm always making mistakes, my dear Georgina!"

"Nonsense!" she refuted swiftly. "You're a most successful man and the *Elysium* is rapidly becoming the most successful theatre in London!"

He swirled the brandy in his glass and studied it intently. "And my private life is a mess," he said soberly.

Georgina was silenced. For he could only be referring to Prudence and the pain that her affair with someone else was causing him. There was nothing she could say or do to ease the heartache and humiliation that she had suffered herself but still did not know how to lessen for him.

Bart knew there had been bitterness in his tone. He knew that she was embarrassed and he regretted the impulsive words. Of course she would suppose that he was hurt by the gossip that linked Prudence and John

Jordan . . . but there had been many rumours about Prudence and other men and he was not in the habit of taking them very seriously and he did not think that this impetuous affair of current interest would do anything but fizzle out very rapidly.

He had merely meant that he was a lonely man — and it was true. He had never known it until that moment but there was a void in his life that he had tried in vain to fill with a succession of women. He was a lonely, dissatisfied and not very happy man. His success with the *Elysium* meant little when compared with the emptiness of his life for who was there who really cared a damn for him and who was there who really mattered to him?

He had friends in plenty but they led their own lives and he played a very small part in their affairs. He had no close family. He had enjoyed the company and the embrace of desirable and lovely and often famous women but he had never been involved in a lasting relationship. His feeling for Prudence had never been the kind of loving that urged a man into marriage although it was possible that he might have drifted into it eventually at her desire. Events had proved that Prudence did not love him any more than he loved her . . . and the knowledge did not hurt. It should hurt, he realised — and knew that the lack was in himself. He had never cared deeply for Prudence or for any woman. He had always cherished his freedom too much to commit himself so irrevocably to caring. Now he understood that the path he had always followed had only led to loneliness . . .

Georgina was silent, aching to offer some kind of comfort and not even daring to stretch out her hand to him.

She was very aware of him, very conscious of his masculine attractiveness in that moment . . . and the knowledge of his pain and disappointment over Prudence was also tugging at her compassion. She warmed to him.

Then she realised that her heart was quickening its beat simply for his nearness . . . and suddenly she took fright.

She put down her untouched sherry. "I still have some work to do," she said lightly. "I ought to be getting on with it." She turned towards the door, caught her high heel in the thickness of the rug and stumbled — and Bart caught her swiftly with a strong, sure hand.

For a moment her lovely face was on a level with his own and he knew the irresistible desire to kiss the mouth that abruptly seemed to very kissable.

Georgina's heart leaped violently at the unmistakable warmth in his eyes and she knew that he meant to kiss her . . . and she was a confusion of delight and dismay!

Bart was master of himself in a moment. He released her with an impersonality that made Georgina wonder if she had only imagined the involuntary tightening of his hand, the flicker of desire in his dark eyes, the breathless moment when she had almost felt the touch of his lips on her own.

"All right . . . ?" he asked carelessly.

She nodded. "Yes, thanks — I caught my heel in the rug," she explained unnecessarily, more coolly than she intended because she was so anxious that he should not suppose she had manoeuvred that brief intimacy.

Bart looked down at her thoughtfully. There was unmistakable reserve in her tone, an unmistakable reluctance to meet his eyes. She was trying hard to maintain the impersonal distance that had always marked their relationship in the past — and his spirits lifted at the implications in the effort.

She was shy in his presence — after all the months of working for him! She was a little wary of him although they had been alone on many occasions and she had never shown the slightest sign of apprehension until now. Either she sensed an alteration in his attitude to

115

herself . . . or she experienced a change in her own attitude! She would be wholly at ease if she were not so sensitive to the atmosphere . . . and Bart was suddenly convinced that she played some part in the creating of that atmosphere. She was just as aware of him as he was abruptly and a little alarmingly aware of her!

It came as a shock to discover the hold she already had over his emotions and he wondered for how long he had been blinding himself to her decided appeal for him. He was a proud man, a sensitive man, and all the evidence indicated that Georgina was fickle and flirtatious and reluctant to commit herself to a permanent relationship with any man — and he would need to be the first and the only in the life of any woman that he allowed himself to love . . .

116

7

GEORGINA went soberly down the stairs, her heart thudding. It had shocked and alarmed her to realise that swift response in her to Bart's physical magnetism. In all the long months since Rennie had held her and murmured his tender lies, all desire had lain dormant. No one had quickened her blood to wanting and heaven knew there had been plenty of men in her life since she had broken with Rennie. Yet that brief, meaningless contact with Bart Blair had disturbed her senses with a rapidity and an intensity that she did not want to recognise . . . or to repeat!

For there was as little future in desiring Bart as there had been in loving and wanting Rennie . . . and she would not be hurt again, she thought defiantly, angrily, bitterly.

She closed her mind to the implications in the entire incident, so trivial
and easily forgettable as it was! After
all, absolutely nothing had happened,
she told herself firmly. Then, with
the honesty that was so characteristic,
she admitted ruefully to herself that
something had happened . . . something
had definitely sparked between them!
It could be nothing more than physical
attraction, of course. Nevertheless, it
was a danger to be avoided. If she
wanted to go on working for Bart
Blair then she must take care to
protect herself from a repetition of
that strangely exhilarating moment.
He had something of a reputation
as a womaniser and she certainly did
not wish to tangle with him! She liked
her job and she liked the man and it
would be a great pity to ruin everything
by fanning that tiny spark of mutual
attraction in any way.

Since her teens Georgina had known
that she quickened desire in most men
without even trying . . . an inexplicable

gift that had led to some difficult and embarrassing moments before she learned how to cope with the inevitable advances. So she had been thankful that Bart had never shown the least sign of being affected by her physical presence during the months that she had worked for him. Yet it was not imagination that for a fleeting moment he had known the same kind of wanting that had surged in her blood — the very air had been electric with the tension of mutual desire!

Almost desperately, she jerked her thoughts from Bart and tried to concentrate on her work . . . and would not even look up when he entered the office on his way backstage.

Bart glanced at that determinedly bent head with a faint smile in his eyes . . . and there was more regret than amusement in the smile. In any other circumstances, he might have followed his instinct and laid siege to her affections . . . but she was his secretary and he had never thought it wise to mix business with pleasure. Besides, he reminded himself ruefully, she was very involved with someone else just now . . . and that was more of a deterrent than any scruple.

Without speaking to her, he collected the things he wanted from his office and went out again . . . and Georgina looked after him with unconscious wistfulness. It was just as well that he meant to be as impersonal as he had always been . . . and yet it would have been rather nice to look upon him as a friend as well as employer. He would be a good friend, she fancied . . . reliable, dependable, thoughtful and considerate, warm and generous and understanding. It would be very easy to warm to him without necessarily visualising him as Rennie's successor in her heart . . .

Bart stood talking to Bryan King, the stage manager. The lights had been fixed and the panic was over and the performance had begun smoothly. The alterations to the script had provided a subtle improvement that he felt would be well received and he was optimistic about the future of the play.

Georgina waited by the stage door for Mathew, chatting to the doorkeeper who was one of her particular favourites. He had been at the theatre for many years and knew many amusing and interesting and sometimes scandalous anecdotes about past and present names in the business. Now he was recalling an incident that concerned her father and a *grande dame* of an actress who had thoroughly deserved to have a scene stolen from her . . . and Georgina's pretty laugh rang out suddenly.

Bryan turned to look at her with instant admiration. "That's a great girl," he commented warmly. "It's no exaggeration to say that we are a happier company for her coming . . . she has a way with her, you know."

Bart raised a sardonic eyebrow, inclined to believe that personal interest more than truth coloured the flattering words. He knew a perverse desire to prick the bubble of Georgina's popularity — but he had no ammunition. She *was* a great girl . . . sweet and warm and good-natured, lively and lovely, thoroughly deserving the liking and admiration she received from everyone and which she never appeared to accept as inevitable despite her obvious awareness of her popularity.

Nothing was ever too much trouble for Georgina and everything was done with a smile and a swift and pleasing readiness. Spirits seemed to lift simply for her presence and problems seemed to dissolve simply for her attention and it seemed that most people made that little extra effort simply to win a smile of approval from his secretary. She was undoubtedly an asset and he would be very sorry to lose her . . . but if she was going to make a habit of tugging unexpectedly at his heart then it might be as well to replace her, he thought wryly.

For months he had felt drawn

towards her, he now admitted. Now, like a foolish, callow youth, he found himself resenting the attentions of every other man around . . . from the elderly doorkeeper to the immature call-boy. He wanted to call Georgina to him and take her off to some quiet place where only he could exist for her. Too many men responded to her loveliness — and he wanted her all to himself and for himself.

He was a little shocked to discover the force of that wanting. He did not believe for a moment that he was in love with his secretary. But the way he felt was disturbing to a man who had always preferred the kind of light, unemotional, undemanding relationship that he had enjoyed with Prudence and others in the past. For he knew that if opportunity offered he would make many demands on Georgina and instinctively give much of himself and he would not want to take second place to anyone or anything in her life. He suddenly suspected that she might easily become the most vital, most precious thing in *his* life . . . surpassing even his feeling for the *Elysium*. Therefore he must be wary for she seemed to have the ability to inspire a man to love — and he did not want to love any woman so wholeheartedly.

The man called Mathew arrived and Georgina drew him eagerly towards her, linked her hand in his arm, smiled up at him with obvious affection and seemed to urge him to listen to the doorkeeper's anecdote. A little abruptly, Bart excused himself and walked away . . . and Bryan had too much claim on his time and attention to wonder at the sudden tightening of the lean jaw, the sudden grimness of the expression in the dark eyes, the sudden and rather obvious impatience in the way he had turned from contemplation of his secretary and her companion . . .

It was Mathew's last evening in London and he was determined to make it a memorable occasion. He swept Georgina from club to club and somehow they met any number of friends and acquaintances en route and somehow they ended up at a party on an island in the middle of the river near Richmond in the early hours of the morning. It turned out that their host was an old friend from Mathew's university days and he was delighted to hear of the coming wedding . . . and Georgina discovered, a little to her amusement, that she was generally regarded as the bride — and lost count of the times that her happiness was toasted by the genial, well-meaning crowd. She did not even attempt to set people right for it did not really matter, she thought indulgently.

She was feeling rather emotional . . . probably because she had drunk a little too much. But she found herself envying the unknown Amanda a little . . . not particularly because she was to marry Mathew but because she was to marry a man she loved and who loved her in return. Mathew was a dear and she was a very fortunate girl, Georgina thought sentimentally. How much she had enjoyed being with him during the all-too-short week! What a grand fellow he was: what a delightful companion; what a loving and lovable friend . . . and how much she was going to miss him, she thought regretfully.

Having him around had emphasised the usual lonely emptiness of her life, she realised. She was very much a loner for all the men that she knew and saw so frequently. None of them were really very important to her and she doubted that she was really very important to any one of them. Oh, it was good to have friends and of course she enjoyed the restaurant and clubs, the visits to theatres and cinemas, the balls and the parties and she loved the constant flow of old and new acquaintances. But one always returned to the little flat and the loneliness that could attack in the night.

With a little sigh, she admitted

that there was something missing . . . something she needed. A man to love her and look after her and be with her always. A man who did not deceive her and desert her and fill her with despair.

There were men in plenty. Without conceit, she knew that she was pretty, pleasing, vivacious, good company and certainly she did not lack for male attention. She was quite fond of one or two of the men she knew . . . but fondness was not loving. There were men who showed signs of real and welcome affection for her . . . but not one who really loved her, she decided wistfully.

She realised that she could not inspire any man to lasting love . . . brief infatuation, fleeting desire, warm liking, affection — but not love. It was a fact of life and she did not mean to lose any sleep over it and yet there were nights when she tossed and turned, restless and unhappy, aching to love and be loved — and wondering if she would ever cease to want Rennie!

It was ridiculous to be still in love with him, she knew. It was foolish beyond measure to go on wanting a man who had shown clearly that his interest was merely sexual and that the chase had been more exciting than the conquest. But Georgina went on loving him and wanting him with every passing day. At the same time, she resented his very existence for while her emotions were so entangled with Rennie it was obviously impossible for her to care for any other man.

Love and hate were thus inextricably mixed in her feeling for the man who had used and discarded her — and sometimes Georgina wondered if there was an old-fashioned insistence in her need to love the man to whom she had given herself to irrevocably. Another girl might have dismissed the affair and decided to forget it in another man's arms. But Georgina went on loving and remembering and sometimes it was hard to differentiate between her feeling for any man who held her close and her feeling for the man who had once held her and kissed away the last murmur of resistance.

She wondered how Rennie had reacted to the much-publicised affair between Prudence Carroll and the American director who was universally known by his surname alone. Not well, she decided. Rennie liked to manoeuvre and manipulate an affair to his satisfaction and end it when *he* pleased . . . and Georgina did not doubt that there had been some kind of an affair in existence between him and Prudence although it might not have gone very far. However it was, it must have been unpalatable to find himself abruptly dropped for another man . . . a rare experience for the personable and supremely confident Rennie, she thought drily.

There seemed to be very little doubt about the relationship between Prudence and Jordan . . . and they apparently did not care that the whole world knew of their delight in each other. Georgina was rather surprised that Prudence had shown so little consideration for Bart's feelings. She had always seemed to be very fond of him and quite determined to marry him one day . . . and yet she had thrown herself into a tempestuous affair with Jordan almost on first meeting if the press could be believed. Georgina, like many others who had never come into contact with him, wondered why Jordan should appeal so forcibly to the beautiful and very selective Prudence . . . so forcibly that she was willing to risk the loss of Bart for the sake of a brief and passionate affair that must burn itself out if only because it was so fierce. Georgina found it impossible to understand that Prudence could prefer any man to Bart. To be loved and wanted by a man like Bart was surely all that any woman could ask, Georgina decided a little wistfully.

It was very late . . . or very early, according to one's view of the matter — when she finally persuaded Mathew to leave the party that was still in full swing. She reminded him firmly that she was a working girl and that he had a plane to catch the following day . . . or, rather, the same day!

Thankfully she tumbled into bed and into sleep to dream confusingly of Bart and Mathew and Rennie so that they merged into one man who waited at the altar while she walked backwards down the aisle in a dress shirt of palest blue and high-heeled shoes, carrying an enormous framed photograph of Prudence in place of a bouquet.

She woke to the pealing of the door bell and lay, still confused, trying to marshal her thoughts and briefly believing that the doorbell was the church bells from her dream.

Mathew was up and about preparing tea and toast with virtually one hand while shaving with the other, moving between tiny bathroom and tiny kitchen with the strategic timing of long practice.

He was startled by the doorbell and narrowly missed nicking his chin with a razor. He swore beneath his breath as the bell pealed again with impatience. He went to the front door of the flat, pausing briefly to catch a slice of toast as it popped out of the toaster . . .

Bart was thankful that it was just a walk of a few minutes to the mansions where Georgina lived from the *Elysium*. He needed her in a hurry. He had been woken by a telephone call from a journalist friend with the disturbing news that Prudence had been involved in a car crash with John Jordan. There were as yet no further details . . . it had merely been a brief newsflash on the French radio. Bart had thanked his friend, made a few necessary telephone calls, showered and shaved in a hurry and kept the radio turned on at volume in case the news with more details had reached the BBC. Then he had set out to collect Georgina who must go with him to France in the private plane he had chartered. He had already arranged for Evelyn to hold the fort at the *Elysium* and to cancel all his appointments for the next few days. He did not know what would meet him on his arrival and he closed his mind to the dark thoughts that leaped but it might be necessary for him to remain in France for some days and he would need his secretary.

He was disconcerted when the door opened to reveal Mathew, wearing nothing but pyjama trousers and a great deal of lather on his face. His eyes hardened abruptly. He had known that Georgina was a flirt but he had fought the suspicion that she might be promiscuous and he was shaken and shocked to realise that the man had obviously spent the night with her.

He said coldly: "I'm sorry to disturb you . . . is Miss Durrell at home?"

Mathew grinned engagingly, recognising him. "Sure . . . come in! She's still in bed, I'm afraid. We made quite a night of it!"

Bart looked at him with dislike.

But he followed him into the small, surprisingly tidy sitting-room. It was his first visit to Georgina's flat and it reflected her personality. It was small but sunny and welcoming, bright and cheerful, pleasantly furnished.

Georgina was instantly roused from the last vestiges of sleep by that familiar voice. She threw off the covers and scrambled into her dressing-gown and appeared at the door of her bedroom with her shining hair tumbling about her shoulders and her pretty face flushed with a mixture of sleep and surprise.

To Bart, she just looked guilty and dismayed — and he was careful not to allow the smallest hint of censure to creep into his expression for it was none of his business how she conducted her private life . . . and he certainly did not mean to reveal the flooding disappointment.

"I hope you'll forgive this intrusion," he said, a little stiffly. "But there seems to be some fault with your telephone . . . I couldn't get through and so I had to come to the flat."

Georgina looked instinctively at the telephone on its small table . . . and recalled that she had left the receiver off the hook after playful calls from friends they had left at the party had disturbed them three times in succession.

"Is anything wrong?" she asked quickly and immediately knew it to be a foolish question for only an emergency of some kind would bring Bart to her flat at half-past eight in the morning. "What is it . . . the theatre?"

"It's Prudence," he said quietly. "There's been some kind of an accident . . . she's hurt."

The colour drained from her face. "Oh no! Bart, is it very bad?" she asked fearfully.

"I don't know. There's some confusion and I can't get any information except that she was in a road accident near Mentone. I'm flying out this morning and I want you to come with me, Georgina . . . is it possible?"

"Of course," she said without hesitation. "My passport is in order. I'll get dressed and pack a few things," she went on with swift practicality. "Will you wait or shall I come down to the theatre?"

"I'll come back for you in an hour," he said and turned away, ignoring Mathew who had retreated to the kitchen to pour a much-needed cup of tea for his cousin and now returned with it.

Georgina went after Bart and laid her hand on his arm, a little shyly. "I'm sure that we'll find Prudence safe and sound," she said gently. "Try not to worry . . . "

He looked down at her. He was angry with her, disappointed in her, near to despising her . . . and yet he warmed to the genuine concern and compassion in her eyes. Briefly he covered the slender hand in his own. "Thanks," he said and smiled — the slow, rich smile that struck unexpectedly at her heart . . .

8

GEORGINA stood on the terrace that overlooked the shore and the calm sea and took a deep, steadying breath. It had been a very stressful day . . . falling into bed in the early hours after that hectic evening, waking to the startled awareness of Bart's voice and the shocking news that he brought, hastily packing, even more hastily parting with Mathew who was now on his way to Johannesburg, driving the seemingly endless miles to the airport with Bart's tense impatience dragging at her own nerves and then the bumpy flight in the small chartered plane across the Channel. They had finally arrived in Mentone to discover the Prudence had escaped unhurt but the John Jordan had been killed outright in the accident.

Prudence allowed herself to be treated

for shock and then had insisted on returning to her villa. And it was there that Bart and Georgina had found her, calm and dry-eyed and cold as marble. Her stillness was terrible. She greeted them without surprise and without interest and looked at Bart blankly when he gently mentioned the fact of Jordan's death.

She was refusing to accept, Georgina thought with compassion. She had cradled the man's lifeless body in her arms until police and ambulance men had arrived and then she had kissed the cold mouth and allowed herself to be led away without protest. She must know that Jordan was dead . . . but she would not, could not accept that he had gone away from her, Georgina thought, her heart swelling with pity for Prudence. She must have loved him very much although they had known each other such a short time. Time had very little to do with loving, after all. They had obviously lived a lifetime of loving in those few, all-too-short days that they had been together.

Bart was with her now, holding the cold hands, talking to her gently despite the lack of response, trying to bring vitality and warmth back to the still, emotionless, expressionless woman that he loved so dearly. Georgina was impressed by the tenderness and the concern and the consideration that he showed for she had seen a side of Bart that she had only suspected to exist. He was incredibly gentle, infinitely kind, loving and tender and warm, knowing just how to cope with the situation, she thought admiringly . . . and felt a tiny pang of most unsuitable envy. She scolded herself fiercely. Surely she did not grudge Prudence the smallest ounce of his attention and consideration at such a time! In any case, she had no right to his attention and consideration at any time, Georgina told herself firmly . . . he was merely her employer and she must be very much of an encumbrance to him at this particular time.

Feeling herself to be an unnecessary

third, she had slipped out to the terrace and she stood there, half-consciously soaking up the warmth of the sun and admiring the beauty of her surroundings, and wondering why Bart had brought her to France with him. Not for moral support even if he had found Prudence to be badly hurt or even dead, she decided . . . a man like Bart did not seem to need anyone. He was strong and forceful and self-sufficient, a man of character and integrity and admirable purpose, a man who stood way above every other man she knew, a man who walked alone and confident through life because he preferred it that way. And yet he loved Prudence, Georgina thought, wondering . . . it was obvious in every look, ever word, every tender gesture and attention. Loved her enough to overlook the passionate affair that had ended so tragically. Loved her enough to hurry to her side when she needed him — to be there even before she knew that she needed him! Loved her enough to stay with her, look after her, surround her with tender concern and compassion and to sacrifice all other considerations to her need. Obviously, nothing mattered more than Prudence and her peace of mind and her happiness and he would do all in his power to secure those things for her if possible.

Georgina looked over the dancing blue waters of the Mediterranean and the tears stole slowly down her cheeks to taste salt on her lips before she was aware of them. She was appalled. Hastily, she brushed a hand across her wet eyes . . . and tried to ignore the implications of the tears that had accompanied her thoughts.

It had been a long and wearisome day. She was overwrought and emotional and there was an indefinable but persistent little ache in her breast. She turned away from the beauty that seemed to have moved her so unbearably . . . and looked directly into Rennie's handsome face.

She had known the inevitability of their meeting. She had almost unconsciously tensed herself for it. She had almost found herself dreading it more than she welcomed it. She had believed it would be a poignant meeting in the circumstances.

Reality was very different to the imagined moment. She looked at Rennie and felt nothing . . . not the smallest lift of her heart, not the slightest degree of delight. Suddenly he was just a man that she did not like or admire very much for all the silver-tongued charm that had once swept her into ecstatic surrender. From the sincere conviction that she loved him to the sure realisation that he meant nothing at all to her was the step of an instant. She looked at Rennie and knew that he was just a small piece of her regretted past and he could not threaten her present and he certainly had no part to play in her future.

"Gina . . . !" he exclaimed, his tone betraying his surprise at seeing her. He had heard of Bart's arrival at the villa but it had not occurred to him that Georgina was with her employer . . . he would not have supposed there was any need for her presence in Mentone. He was surprised into renewed appreciation of her prettiness as she turned towards him. Abruptly he felt the quickening of the former desire for her and wondered why he had thought himself weary of her loveliness and quiet appeal. He went towards her, slowly, giving himself time to shape his approach and giving her time to respond once more to the impact of his smiling charm. "Gina," he said again, caressingly, intimately. "It really *is* you — and I thought you were a mirage, born of my thought of you!"

She smiled faintly, amused by the blatant extravagance of a claim that could have no foundation in truth. "You haven't given me a thought in months," she returned lightly, indifferently.

Rennie felt the old excitement rising. For she was not going to fall swiftly and too easily into his arms this time, he realised. She was wary, suspicious, resisting the charm which had once overwhelmed her . . . and it was a challenge that he could not resist.

"Not true," he said softly, vibrantly. "You don't know how often I've thought of you — and remembered . . . and regretted." He stood very close to her, waiting for some sign of the inevitable response. "I've missed you, Gina . . . even more than I realised," he added with the engaging smile that usually went straight to a woman's heart.

This time, it completely missed its target. Georgina looked at him, unsmiling, unaffected by him, marvelling that she had supposed him to be the epitome of all her dreams. The love she had felt for this man was only rainbow gold, after all . . . something that did not exist outside her foolish dreams. He was a mass of conceit, she thought critically. No doubt he thought that he had only to smile, to murmur a great deal of nonsense, and she would melt once more into his arms. Perhaps he regarded her arrival as heaven-sent . . . a sure balm for the knock to his pride that Prudence had lost interest in him as soon as John Jordan came into her life. For Rennie could not have liked the man's easy conquest of a woman he wanted for himself . . .

Bart paused by the open window that overlooked the terrace. He stood for the briefest of moments before moving away, a little abruptly . . . but it was long enough for him to recognise the intent in the man's expression and the response in Georgina as she looked up at him. They were very close and Bart did not doubt the invitation and the encouragement that she offered or Rennie Bruce's readiness to respond.

She was insatiable, he thought furiously. It seemed that every man who crossed her path was seen as grist to her mill! No man was safe from her provocative smile, the warm invitation in her eyes, the unmistakable encouragement in the way she lifted her face to be kissed. Flirtation he could forgive for she was young and pretty and perhaps flattered by the attention that came her way. But she was more than just a flirt, he had discovered to his fierce disappointment and regret. She had a very sensual nature and she obviously set out to excite desire, to encourage it and to respond with eager delight — and he had unpalatable proof that she would not hesitate to spend her nights with the man of the moment.

Fiercely he crushed the weakness within him that was kin to loving. She was not worth the glow of warmth, that kindling of tenderness, that insistent ache to have and to hold, to protect and cherish, to surround with all the happiness that heaven might allow.

He recalled the moment when he had held her, that pretty face so close to his own, and known the longing to kiss her, enfold her in his arms. He had sensed her willingness to be held and kissed and known she would respond with a sweetness that might easily transform the entire meaning of his life. He was thankful now that he had been strong enough to resist her impact on his emotions and instincts. For he was only on the threshold of loving and he could step back as easily as forward, he told himself confidently. Loving Georgina was not inevitable, after all! . . . and it was a mistake that a man could not afford to make if he wanted any peace of mind in the future!

He went back to Prudence who sat in the high winged chair, hands linked loosely in her lap, eyes wide but unseeing. She was a beautiful statue, frozen with grief . . . and she needed him. Bart loved her dearly and he was determined to thrust Georgina out of his mind and heart for ever for the sake of Prudence who must not be hurt again.

He spoke to her but she did not hear him for Jordan's voice was echoing in her heart and mind with the declaration of his love. She looked at Bart but only Jordan was before her eyes . . . that lean, sensitive, handsome face with its proud nose and intelligent brow and sensual, humorous mouth. She was not aware of her surroundings for she saw only the rolling scenario of days spent with Jordan . . . days of living life to the very full, of tasting heaven in advance, of loving and knowing herself loved. Bart leaned down and covered both her cold hands with his own in gentle reassurance but it was not his touch that she felt for memory was strong within her for the urgent yet tender hands that had held and caressed her and expressed so much loving.

They loved and they were one, complementing each other in every way, loving as others had never loved or known how to love, belonging wholly and eternally to each other, living only for each other. Now she was told that Jordan was dead but it could not be true for Jordan was a strong, dynamic, vital force that could not be so easily extinguished. She was told that Jordan was dead but that would mean an end to their loving — and how could there be an end to loving such as theirs? His physical presence might have gone from her but she knew that he was with her still and always would be because their love was eternal and eternity was a world of love.

It was all so clear and so logical to her that Prudence was irritated by the compassion that was being heaped upon her. Why should people be sorry for her when she knew that she would never again be alone or lonely or unloved for Jordan's love would surround her and protect her for ever. Nothing could change the love they had known and would always know for each other. Nothing could erase the precious moments that they had shared. How could she grieve for something she had not lost and could never lose because Jordan's love was not something that ended with his life.

But she could not make Bart or anyone else realise that she did not need the pity and the comforting. Everyone thought she was grieving when she merely wanted to be left alone to remember, to relive and to rejoice that she had met and recognised and claimed her destiny before it was too late. At least she had known the precious gift of mutual and very joyful loving and few were so blessed.

A little shudder rippled through her slender body and then she sighed once, softy . . . and gently set aside memory for the present.

She became aware of Bart, leaning over her so anxiously, loving concern in his eyes. She smiled, reassuring him. "I'm all right, Bart," she said quietly. "Quite all right." She patted his hand in a little gesture of comfort for she was sorry that he should have been so upset and alarmed and she understood that he had been sick with dread until he discovered that she was virtually unhurt.

It had been a freak accident. Driving towards Mentone at speed with Prudence beside him in the fast sports car, Jordan had been unexpectedly confronted by a transcontinental lorry that had skidded on an oil patch and ended up straddling the road. He had slammed on the brakes, jerking the car to a brutal halt and, while Prudence had been saved from serious injury by the seat belt he had insisted she wear, he had been thrown against the steering wheel and the hammer blow to his heart had killed him instantly.

Bart searched her beautiful face, wondering. Her stillness had disturbed him. She had been in shock and he had dreaded her reactions when she woke to true realisation of the tragedy. But she *was* all right, he realised thankfully — and knew her too well to make the mistake that many were to make of supposing her feeling for John Jordan to have been superficial simply because she appeared to recover swiftly from the tragic loss of her lover. Bart knew instinctively that her emotions had been deeply touched by that brief interlude and he sensed that while she meant to show a brave face to the world she would continue to mourn in secret for the one man who had inspired her to real loving.

He took her lovely face between his two hands and kissed her on the brow. "My brave girl," he said gently.

She looked at him steadily, quite composed. Dear Bart. He was so anxious, so concerned, so loving. He was a true friend, she thought with gratitude, impressed by his arrival at the villa within hours of the accident despite the many demands on his time and attention. It was heart-warming to know that he cared so much and wanted to be with her at a time when he knew that she would need him. He understood her so well.

He and Jordan would have liked each other, she felt. They were alike in many ways and there had been moments when she had been faintly puzzled by a certain familiarity with Jordan's personality until she realised that there were certain facets that reminded her of Bart. Perhaps it explained why she had been so sure that she cared for Bart until she met Jordan . . . perhaps she would have continued to love the shadow if she had never known the substance!

"I'm so glad you came," she said quietly. "Take me home, Bart."

"Yes, I will, my darling," he said tenderly. "But not immediately, I'm afraid." He hesitated and then went on reluctantly: "There has to be an inquest . . ."

"And I'm needed as a witness? Yes, of course," she said matter-of-factly. "Then the funeral . . . I must attend."

"That isn't necessary," Bart said swiftly. "Everyone will understand that it will be too much of an ordeal for you . . . you've had a terrible shock and a nasty shake-up, Prudence. I think we should leave for home as soon as the inquest is over."

She shrugged. "Very well. Let the world think what it likes," she said, a little bleakly. She rose from her chair. "Suddenly I feel very tired, Bart. I think I'll go to my room and rest."

"Would you like Georgina to go with you?" he asked thoughtfully, doubting that she ought to be alone just now.

"Georgina . . . ? Oh yes, you brought her with you, didn't you?" she recalled without interest. "No, I don't need Georgina. Ellen will look after me very well," she added, referring to the maid-cum-dresser-cum-companion who was more friend than employee. "I'm afraid I shall be poor company for a little while, Bart — so you and Georgina must amuse each other." She moved slowly, a little stiffly, towards the door. "I'm beginning to feel the bruises now," she said wryly. "In more ways than one . . . "

"Prudence!" He said her name impulsively, urgently and, as she turned, added: "I'll always be here, you know . . . whenever you want me."

She nodded. "Thank you, darling," she said with the first warmth she had shown since his arrival. "You're so reliable . . ."

As the door closed behind Prudence, Bart turned to the table with its array of bottles and glasses and poured himself a stiff drink. He sat down in a deep armchair and reviewed the day with all its dread and dismay and disappointment. He felt weary and drained and dispirited and the brandy did nothing to dispel his mood.

He looked round but did not bother to rise when Georgina and Rennie Bruce entered from the terrace. He bestowed a curt nod on the man that he had met a few times and never liked.

"I came to see Prudence . . . Miss Carroll — to offer my sympathy and see if there is anything I can do for her," Rennie said, disconcerted by the hostility in Bart's eyes which he attributed to resentment of the warm friendship he had enjoyed with

Prudence before John Jordan captivated her interest so completely. "How is she now?"

"Very shaken, naturally. She's resting at the moment. But I'll tell her that you called and I'm sure she will appreciate your kind thought." Bart was brusque and did not care that his dislike showed. He looked coldly at the young man who was so obviously an egotist . . . and looked even more coldly on Georgina who stood by Bruce's side, unsmiling but with a faint flush in her cheeks and a decided sparkle in her lovely eyes. Flirtation became her, he thought drily . . . she was never prettier than at such moments.

Rennie knew himself dismissed and had no choice but to take his leave . . . but he very much resented the high-handed attitude that Bart Blair had adopted as though he had the right to protect Prudence from an invasion of her privacy at this time.

9

RENNIE was fuming. He was silent until he reached his car and then he turned on Georgina, furious. "Damn him! He had no right to take that tone with me!" he declared passionately. "What the devil does he mean by sending me away like an impertinent schoolboy!"

Georgina looked at him steadily. He was flushed with anger and looked very young and oddly vulnerable. She could not help feeling a little sorry for him. Bart had slapped him down quite unmistakably and he had already suffered the humiliation of being dropped by Prudence when John Jordan came on the scene. Perhaps it was a salutary experience after the way he had behaved towards her and other women in the past but Georgina could not be vindictive and her warm heart melted

157

with swift compassion. She knew him to be very sensitive as well as proud and certainly Bart had been rough with him.

"Oh, it wasn't quite like that," she said gently, soothing his wounded pride. "Bart was rather curt but I'm sure he didn't mean to offend you, Rennie. It's just that he's been under a great deal of strain today and his only concern is for Prudence, you know," she added fairly.

"And mine!" he said swiftly. "I'm extremely fond of her . . . most upset by this business! It has hit her hard, of course. She was very infatuated with Jordan. The affair couldn't have lasted but it's tragic that it should end in this way. I'm deeply sorry for Prudence and I want to tell her so personally . . . "

"Come again tomorrow," Georgina suggested sensibly. "I'm sure she will want to see you then . . . after all, you are a friend."

"A close friend," he said meaningfully . . . and then remembered that he was talking to Georgina and that it might not suit his book to emphasise the closeness of his friendship with Prudence, after all. "I don't mean to imply that we were ever lovers, of course," he added lightly. "I'm fond of her and I admire her tremendously and I believe she had something to do with my being offered the part in the film and I'm grateful . . . but our friendship was just that and nothing more no matter what you might have heard, Gina, my sweet." He smiled down at her, his good humour returning as he realised that the first coldness, more defensive than determined, was melting. He had her sympathy and that might be the first step towards a renewal of their former relationship.

He looked into the lovely eyes that met his so squarely, so coolly . . . and something happened to him. Something totally unexpected. He had supposed her easily dismissed, easily forgotten, like all the other women in his life. He had not once regretted breaking with her during the past year and there had been no stirring of interest at any of their occasional, inevitable meetings . . . and yet now, without rhyme or reason, he was very much aware of her and urgent to possess her once more and convinced that she was more important to his happiness than he had realised until that moment.

He had said as much earlier in the evening, the words tripping lightly from his tongue with the careless insincerity he had brought to all his affairs — and yet perhaps this time he had meant the sentiment all unconsciously. For the cold indifference in her attitude struck deep at the very heart of him and now he discovered that he was anxious for her liking and affection and respect as much as for the sweetness of her lips and the warm delights to be found in her arms.

His attitude to women had always been very casual, very careless. He had never thought that he would want a lasting relationship with any woman.

Yet this sudden desire for Georgina was very much more than sexual and she abruptly seemed to be all that any man could want in a woman for the rest of his life.

He said quietly, earnestly: "You know, there's no one like you, Gina. No one to compare with you. Giving you up was the biggest mistake of my life."

Georgina was staggered by the unmistakable sincerity in his tone. She stared in astonishment for she would have thought him the last person to admit to a mistake of any kind. She was stunned by the words, by the warmth and tenderness behind them, by their meaning. In all that long and lonely year, she had ached with love for him, dreamed and despaired, longed for just this moment and just those words . . . and now it was all rainbow gold, dust in her hands, empty and meaningless and misplaced.

"I don't think you mean that, Rennie," she said slowly, carefully.

"You've been hurt, I think — and perhaps you regret having hurt me. Perhaps it seems at the moment that we might comfort each other a little. But it isn't a good idea. I don't really mean anything to you any more."

"Allow me to know how I feel, Gina," he said, a little roughly. He put his arms about her and drew her close, too swiftly for protest. He kissed her, his mouth hard and urgent and demanding.

Her lips parted beneath that kiss but her heart was firmly closed to him. This should have been a most wonderful moment in her life . . . instead she was numb and shocked and a little dismayed to discover that she was utterly dead inside where he was concerned. This was Rennie who held her in his arms and kissed her . . . the man she had firmly believed that she loved and would always love. This was Rennie who incredibly regretted parting with her and wanted her once more — and the miracle she had longed for, prayed for, never really dared to dream could come true, left her untouched and unthankful.

"I've missed you so much," he murmured against her lips, his arms tightening fiercely about her slim waist. "My lovely, lovely girl . . . say that you forgive me! Let's begin again, Gina — I need you!"

Georgina shook her head firmly and pulled herself out of his arms. "I'm sorry Rennie," she said slowly and suddenly her lips quivered with the memory of past pain, past disappointment. "I could never trust you again . . ."

"Oh, my darling!" The words wrenched from him in despair. Then he said quietly, painfully: "I deserve that, of course. I behaved abominably. It was my mistake and I guess I must pay for it . . . but there'll never be anyone but you for me, Gina. I know that now."

She could not doubt that he meant the words, astonishing though they seemed. Her warm heart was moved with swift compassion for him. She

163

could not bear to hurt anyone, could not bear to think of anyone suffering as she had suffered, could not turn away from his pain even if it was his own fault.

Her thoughts and feelings were in a tumult of confusion as she looked at his handsome, troubled face and saw the unhappy regret in his eyes. Was it possible to have stopped loving him so completely when she had been so sure that she would love him for ever? Was it perhaps an unconscious perversity, some foolish instinct for revenge, that insisted she did not want him now that he had so suddenly, so unexpectedly, decided that he wanted her? He had been everything to her for so long . . . how could he suddenly be nothing at all? He was offering her a second chance of happiness with him and it might be wrong to turn it down simply because she no longer knew what she wanted. This might be only a temporary lack of feeling for him — and what if she turned him away only to discover that she did love him, after all?

Impulsively she caught his hands and he turned swiftly, instant hope leaping to his eyes. "Help me, Rennie," she said tremulously. "I don't know what I feel any more . . . "

He gripped her hands so tightly that she felt the tiny bones must break but he was not even aware that she winced. "One small chance — that's all I ask," he said tensely. "I don't expect you to forgive and forget in a moment but you *were* fond of me and perhaps it isn't all dead." He smiled a little shakily. "There must have been something about me that you loved — and could love again!" He raised her hands to his lips and kissed them, one after the other, with a humility that sat oddly on the shoulders of this arrogant, handsome, conceited man. "Give me one day to prove that we could be happy together, Gina," he suggested quietly. "One day . . . is that so much to ask?"

Georgina went slowly into the house as the car roared away down the drive. Her heart was thudding and his words were echoing in her ears. It all seemed so strange, so bewildering, such a sudden change of heart on his part . . . and yet it was no stranger than the sudden change of heart she had known — from loving to not loving in a moment!

She had promised to give him the day he wanted and agreed to be ready to go out with him when he came in the morning . . . but she was not sure that it was a wise decision. For suddenly they seemed to have nothing in common and all she felt for him was a compassion that had been singularly lacking in his attitude towards her when he broke off their relationship.

Bart tossed off his third brandy as she came into the room. She had taken her time in seeing Bruce from the premises, he thought coldly . . . and did not need to wonder how and why it had taken so long. She was a girl who took immediate advantage of her opportunities, after all.

"Another conquest," he said mocking. "How do you do it, Georgina? Is it a gift . . . or a result of long practice?"

She smiled absently, her thoughts more with Rennie and that shattering encounter than with her employer. "I think I just like people and it shows," she said lightly, scarcely registering that his words were a sneer. "But Rennie isn't a new conquest . . . I've known him for a long time. We were at RADA together." Suddenly a little frown crept into her eyes. Perhaps it was something in the way he regarded her with that slightly mocking disapproval in his expression. "I don't know that I like that word, anyway . . . I don't look upon any man as a *'conquest'*," she said, with a hint of annoyance in her tone. "Rennie Bruce is a friend of mine."

"And you have lots of *friends*," he said drily and the slight emphasis on the last word was almost offensive.

Georgina looked at him steadily. "Yes," she said levelly. "I do."

He nodded. "Take care that you don't burn your fingers," he said abruptly. "Playing with fire is a dangerous game."

"They are *my* fingers," she said quietly after a moment's hesitation, a moment's shocked surprise at his interest in her affairs.

He rose to his feet. "Yes, of course. Do you mean to change for dinner, Georgina? I thought we might eat on the terrace as it's such a lovely evening. Prudence is having a tray in her room."

She was grateful that an awkward moment was passed over so easily. She did not know what had prompted that little exchange which was so unlike him. "That sounds very nice," she said lightly. "Yes, I should like to change out of this suit into something cool . . . but I won't keep you waiting too long for your dinner. Give me ten minutes!"

He raised an amused eyebrow. "Impossible! No woman can dress in ten minutes!"

"Now that's a deliberate provocation!" she declared, her eyes dancing as she took up the challenge in the words.

He smiled, finding it quite impossible to go on being angry and disapproving. She was enchanting and delightful and appealing . . . too young and too lovely to be as black as she seemed to want to paint herself, he thought wryly. It was strange that she invoked that oddly Puritan reaction in him. He had never before cared how many lovers a woman had known as long as he was the one and only while the affair lasted. But he could not bear to think of Georgina involved in casual and promiscuous love affairs and a black mood descend on him at the mere thought of her enjoying the kisses and caresses and passionate embrace of other men. He had no right to object to her way of life. He had no right to the kisses that she gave so readily to others and he was not even sure that he wished to establish a right. He merely knew that she had a very disturbing effect on his emotions and he would prefer that she did not flaunt her flirtations under his nose . . .

Georgina smiled back, thinking how very handsome he was and how much charm he possessed when he smiled in just that particular way. Any woman might be forgiven for losing her heart and her head where he was concerned. For he was not just handsome and charming and extremely attractive. He was a man of integrity and character and warmth of heart. He was a man to like and admire and respect and rely upon at all times. He was a man to love even, she thought with an odd little bump of her heart . . .

She showered and towelled herself dry and zipped herself into a clinging silk jersey gown of slate blue that was high at the throat and long in the sleeve, wide-pleated over the firm young breasts and narrow-pleated in the long, hip-hugging skirt. She swept her blonde curls into an elegant knot on the nape of her neck, applied powder and lipstick to the youthfully lovely face that needed neither and hastily touched a perfume stick to her ears and throat and wrists. And even while she sought to look her most attractive she resolutely denied that she set out to appear desirable in Bart Blair's eyes.

She went towards him with a heavily thudding heart, conscious of her extreme prettiness and glad of it if it might make Bart look upon her less coldly, less disapprovingly. He stood in the hall, waiting, studying his watch, tall and very handsome in the dark evening clothes and gleaming white linen . . . and a little smile flickered about his lips as he heard her quick step.

"He looked up, saying: "*Eleven* minutes . . . I told you it was impossible!" He met her eyes and his lips were suddenly dry and a strange contraction hurt his heart. For she was lovely, perfection, smiling at him with something of shyness in her eyes and Bart ached to catch her close, to hold her against his heart, savour the sweetness and the delight and the warmth that was the essence of the woman he loved.

For he loved Georgina. He admitted it to himself at last. For all her faults, her waywardness, her fickle and flirtatious heart, her wilful disregard of everything but what she wanted in life, he loved her deeply and he wanted her with every fibre of his being. He loved her as he had never thought it possible to love any woman. Wanting her was a physical pain. The need to touch her was urgent within him and he went towards her, slowly, hand outstretched.

Georgina hesitated and then she put her hand into his clasp . . . and such a small, slender, touchingly fragile hand it seemed to him.

"A woman may surely be a minute late," she said as lightly as she could for the tumult in her blood at his touch, at the look in his eyes, at his thrilling nearness.

"You may be as late as you like, Georgina," he said and her name was an endearment, a caress, so soft was his voice and so meaningful his tone. "Your kind of beauty is worth a lot of any man's time."

A little flush of pleasure stole into her pretty face. "Such flattery, Mr. Blair," she rebuked laughingly, taking refuge in levity because her heart was plunging in her breast like a wild thing and she was terrified of betraying the effect he had upon her.

"If you don't know that you're beautiful then you must suppose your mirror to be a liar, Miss Durrell," he returned, smiling, tucking her hand firmly into his arm so that she should not slip away from him.

He looked down at her, wanting to kiss her and yet afraid to rush his fences and dreading a possible rebuff. It might be very easy to sweep her off her feet and into his arms . . . but it was much more likely to be difficult to impress upon her that his need of her was different to that of other men. She was not a naïve innocent, after all. She knew men and he had proof that she was experienced and he was not at all sure that she found him attractive. There might be a certain response in her to his admiration, his desire, his need — but no more than she might feel for any man who paid her flattering attention, perhaps.

Georgina knew that little prickle of wariness that always touched her spine where he was concerned . . . perhaps because it would be dangerously easy to lift her face for his kiss, melt into his arms, give gladly all that he might ask of her. The merest touch could heighten her senses and invoke a delicious wanting, such was his physical magnetism. But she was wholly determined to avoid that kind of involvement. Not simply because she worked for him and she liked her job and it would lead to unwelcome complications but because he would demand of her the heart she had determined never to lose again to any man.

Bart Blair was all that she most admired and most liked in a man . . . and she could love him so much if she once allowed her heart to weaken in its resolution, she thought ruefully. But loving him would not bring her any joy, any happiness, any peace of mind . . . for many women had apparently loved him and only one had inspired him to loving in return. No one, having seen him with Prudence that very day, tender and kind and compassionate, could doubt that he loved with all his heart and in just the way that every woman must yearn to be loved, Georgina thought wistfully . . . and knew there was no real place in his affections or his life for her no matter how much he might admire her or briefly desire her . . .

10

SHE was so pretty, so gay, such a delight to him, Bart thought tenderly, smiling at Georgina across the table without caring that all his heart might be in his eyes.

It was a romantic setting . . . like a stage set or a scene from a novel, Georgina decided wryly. The soft hushing of the Mediterranean lapping against the shore and a mellow moon creeping across the sky: dinner for two and candles on the table and huge banks of exotic flowers in the background; wine sparkling in the glass and admiration shining out of his blue eyes and her own heart surely betraying her with every glance, every tremulous smile. Perhaps it was the night or perhaps it was the wine or perhaps it was simply the nearness of him but she was very close to throwing all caution to the winds. Her heart was throbbing . . . and to camouflage its heavy beat she was talking too much, laughing too much. But he seemed to be interested, amused, entertained . . . and she wanted to hold that interest, keep him amused, sustain his obvious enjoyment of her company. Most of all, she wanted him to go on smiling into her eyes with that little glow in the depths of his own eyes that warmed and quietened her so-foolish heart.

She knew that she could make him forget everything but the delight to be found in her embrace. She knew that he wanted her with an urgency that matched her own. She also knew that the kind of loving they might share had very little to do with the kind of loving she ached to know. She would be only a brief interlude . . . as forgettable as all the rest, she thought bleakly. Prudence would still be the only woman of real importance in his life — and her heart contracted with a shaft of agony as she realised why she had always envied and disliked and resented the other woman. She had wanted Bart from the very first moment of meeting him . . . and she had been blinded by her determination to believe herself in love with a man who had cheated and deceived her. Perhaps she had continued to cling to the belief that she loved Rennie because it was a protection against loving Bart. For surely she must always have known that loving Bart was to invite a pain and despair that far surpassed anything she had ever felt because of Rennie's default.

Loving Bart had been inevitable, she suddenly knew . . . and so she had fought it with all her might. She had continued to resist the instinctive knowledge that she loved him . . . but all that resistance had been so much wasted effort. For she had been destined to love him . . . just as he was destined to love Prudence, she thought bleakly.

All in a moment, with the thought

of Prudence, came recollection of what had brought them to this place with all its insidious enchantment that could make her forget everything but Bart's nearness and her longing to steal into his arms and invite his kiss. The bright sparkle of conversation and the lilt of easy laughter suddenly seemed very out of place.

Bart raised a quizzical eyebrow as her expression changed so comically. "What is it?" he asked softly.

"Conscience," she said wryly. "We are a callous pair, Bart! Do you suppose that Prudence can hear us enjoying ourselves so thoroughly?"

He laid his hand on her arm and allowed his fingers to caress the warm, velvety skin on the inside of her wrist. "Prudence is much too generous to resent the fact that life goes on for other people," he assured her confidently.

The soft caress was almost unbearably sensual. A tiny shudder rippled through Georgina . . . and then she jerked her hand from his touch as though it burned. "Shouldn't you check that she's all right? She might be expecting you, Bart . . . we've sat ages over our meal, you know. The candles are burning very low."

"Dismissing me, Georgina?" he said with a wry little smile. He pushed back his chair and rose. "Very well . . . I'll go and see if she needs me. But don't run away. I thought we might go for a stroll along the beach if that appeals to you?" He did not wait for an answer and Georgina realised that it had been more of a dictate than a suggestion.

She looked after him with a rueful little smile in her eyes. If she had any sense at all she would escape to her room and stay there until the magic of the night vanished with the dawn. But she was too much in love to be sensible. For whatever reason, for however fleeting the need, Bart wanted to be with her beneath the moon . . . and it might be the only happiness she might ever know with him. Madness or not, she meant to seize the opportunity that offered to know his kiss, however light and meaningless . . .

He was back very soon. "All well," he reported. "Prudence is asleep . . . nature's own balm for her particular hurt."

Georgina turned from contemplation of the still, moonlit water. "She loved him very much, didn't she?" she said slowly, echoing her thoughts rather than meaning to twist the knife in his wound.

Bart was silent for a moment. Then he said quietly: "Yes, I think so."

"You spoke of her generosity — I think *you* are the most generous person I've ever known," she said impulsively. "She gave so little thought to your feelings and yet you rush to be with her the moment she needs you."

He smiled. "That's friendship," he said lightly but he was touched by the genuine warmth in her voice.

"That's loving," she returned, a little shakily.

"Yes," he agreed readily and might have added that there were many degrees of loving and almost as many interpretations of the emotion that touched human lives so closely. But he did not know how important it was that Georgina should understand how and why he loved Prudence or that it was a very different love to the one that he now knew that he felt for her . . .

Georgina walked beside him on the firm sand, their hands lightly linked in friendship. She was very much at ease with him now where she had been excited and a little apprehensive and even tense. For as they walked, they talked of many things and she gained a new insight into his character . . . the serious, dedicated side of a man who took little from life and gave back so much. In that brief hour, she understood why every instinct had urged her to love him — and she discovered a warmth and a strength and a richness of personality that made her love him all the more.

Real loving was not just the physical urge of a woman for one particular man, after all . . . although sex was an important and very precious part of loving. Loving as she loved Bart was friendship and liking and respect and affection and warming to the same things and speaking the same language, knowing and understanding his thoughts and feelings because they seemed to match her own so well. It was wanting to be with him for the rest of life, loving and caring and sharing the laughter and the tears. It was a certain response to his need — and a need that found satisfaction in his swift, sure response. It was the happiness and the contentment and the comfort to be found in the simple linking of hands, the quiet exchange of glances, a certain smile. It was the way she felt and would always feel about Bart . . . but all his loving was for Prudence and his present need of her was simply the mood of the moment, born of the moonlight and the magic of their lovely surroundings and that inexplicable something in herself that could only bring a man to the verge of loving and never beyond, she thought wryly.

Bart drew her down to sit beside him on a flat slab of rock. He brought his case from his pocket and busied himself with lighting a cigarette. Georgina looked at his handsome face illumined in the flame of the lighter and knew a swift surge of longing and loving. Without conscious thought, only feeling, she leaned towards him and impulsively pressed her lips to his lean cheek. He turned his head to look at her, searching her eyes . . . and then he tossed away the cigarette and reached for her with a little aching murmur of her name.

He held her, hard against his heart, staring over her head at the rippling blackness of the sea, struggling with the feelings she invoked and wondering if he was the world's worst fool to love a girl who was so light of heart that she delighted in adding to her long list of conquests. She was utterly desirable, incredibly lovely, wholly enchanting . . . and much too generous, he thought with a stirring of anger. For the readiness with which she slipped into his arms was a painful reminder that other men had held and kissed her and known the delights that she now seemed to be offering to him without hesitation.

Impatient, Georgina raised her face and tightened her arms about his neck and nestled even closer to him and said his name, softly yet urgently, wanting his kiss and his nearness and some small sign that his need of her was not wholly sexual . . . and she did not realise that invitation was in every line of her lovely body and husky in her voice and bright in her eyes. She loved and she needed to express that love as it welled up so strongly in her slight being . . . and it no longer seemed to matter if she betrayed the way she felt about him although he did not and never could love her in return. For there was no room for pride in her full heart . . .

Bart touched his lips to her hair, pale in the moonlight, soft and scented, escaping from the knot to curl in little, pretty tendrils about her face. He was very tense and the strain was showing in his eyes for he wanted her desperately and he was determined that the surging desire should not be his master.

Georgina did not understand why he would not kiss her when he must know that she ached for the touch of his lips. She did not understand why he merely held her with arms of steel . . . held her so close against his hard, unyielding body that he bruised her breasts. She tried to look into the eyes that avoided her gaze and her heart sank as she saw his grim expression. In an impulsive attempt to soften stone, she kissed him with her heart throbbing on her lips.

Then the floodgates burst abruptly and Bart kissed her savagely, brutally, punishing her for that terrible weakness within himself. His kiss was urgent, demanding . . . and to Georgina it seemed to contain only a fierce and frightening passion. For the first time in her experience, she knew that she had completely lost control of the situation. Bart was a mature and experienced man and he was very determined. She loved him and she wanted him . . . but not like this, she thought in sudden panic, struggling to free herself. Not without a single word of love! Not without tenderness and consideration! She had given herself gladly to Rennie, believing that they loved each other, and he had been the first and the only man in her life. Deeply in love with Bart, desiring only his happiness, how gladly she would have given herself to him in return for one small sign of affection of tenderness. But the very urgency of his silent, tense love-making turned her to ice . . . and she fought him with all the strength in her slender body.

Bart came to his senses all in a

moment and thrust her away with a little groan. He moved away and was still, battling for supremacy of his body, and after a moment or two the tension left him and his heart slowed its painful pounding. He took out cigarettes and would not look at the girl who had swept him almost to the point of no return. She had struck a fierce blow at his pride . . . much more, she had hurt him deeply with her fear and obvious revulsion at the tidal wave of emotion that had possessed him. He was furious with her — and even more angry with himself.

Georgina was too upset even for tears. For she was entirely to blame — and he would never forgive her! She had encouraged him in full awareness of the emotions she evoked . . . and then taken fright like a silly schoolgirl when his feelings got out of hand. Heaven knew what he must be thinking of her . . . but it could only be mild in comparison with her opinion of herself!

"I'm sorry . . . " she stumbled in a small, choked voice. He did not answer. "Bart, I'm sorry," she said again, desperately.

"You might have had more cause to be sorry," he said coldly.

She coloured, understanding. "You wouldn't have forced me," she said swiftly, confidently.

He looked at her then, astonished by her naïvety. "I wish I shared your confidence," he said drily. "I warned you about playing with fire, Georgina."

She said nothing. In silence, he smoked . . . and she sat, staring at hands clenched fiercely in her lap, misery churning in her breast that cold dislike should so swiftly have replaced warm liking. The silence became too much to bear at last and she blurted, near to tears: "Everything is spoiled . . . everything!"

He spun his cigarette into the sea. "Yes," he agreed uncompromisingly. "It seems a pity. My fault, of course . . . it's always been my policy not to mix business with pleasure and it was foolish to forget it. A man should never make love to his secretary — even if she's willing."

Every cold, slightly contemptuous word struck her heart, emphasising that there was not an ounce of love in his feeling for her and that he deeply regretted becoming even briefly involved with her and that there was no future at all in caring for him.

Consumed by his own pain, Bart wanted to hurt her . . . and felt that only contempt could penetrate the armour of a heart that was light and fickle and careless. He glanced towards her and saw tears on her cheek, wet and gleaming in the moonlight. Anger and pain and hurt pride refused to allow him to reach out, to wipe away the tears with a gentle hand, to put matters right with a kind word.

He scrambled to his feet. "Come on . . . we can't sit here all night," he said abruptly. "You're getting cold."

"I'm not cold and I might want to

sit here all night," she returned tautly. "I know my way back . . . there's no need to wait for me."

He exclaimed sharply: "Don't be childish, Georgina! Do you imagine that I'd leave you on a deserted beach in the middle of nowhere! Give me your hand . . ."

"I can manage," she said brightly and rose, brushing the sand from her skirts. The tears had dried on her cheeks and her face felt stiff and her heart was sore but she stepped out with him with her head held high. Glancing at her, Bart fancied there was a hint of defiance in the tilt of her chin . . . and discovered that she was a stranger to him, after all. She walked in silence, her expression stony, arms folded across her breast as though she felt the cold from the little breeze that had sprung up from nowhere. Without a word, he took off his jacket and draped it about her shoulders. She accepted the gesture with a stiff murmur of thanks . . . and knew her heart contract in anguish. He was so kind, so thoughtful and considerate . . . even though she had probably alienated him for ever with her stupid behaviour. "What happens now?" she asked abruptly. "We can't just carry on as though nothing has happened."

"Nothing *has* happened," he reminded her brusquely. "No thanks to you, I might add."

She winced. "That's just what I mean!" she declared passionately. "You won't forget or forgive — and nor will I! I can't continue to work for you in that kind of atmosphere!"

He shrugged as though it did not matter but his heart shrank at the thought that she might walk out of his life as untouched by any real feeling for him as on the day that she had entered it. "In the circumstances, I agree with you," he said tautly. "But I shall be sorry to part with you, Georgina . . . good secretaries are like gold dust these days."

Another stab of pain — and she wondered if he deliberately set out to hurt and could not blame him if he did. His anger and contempt were wholly justified, after all . . . she knew just how men regarded the kind of girl who led them on with deliberate provocation only to cry off at the last moment. It had not really been like that at all but it must seem so to Bart and how could she explain her feelings to a man so cold and distant and uncaring?

How right her instinct had been to warn her against becoming involved with him, she thought bleakly. It had led to exactly what she had feared . . . heartache and humiliation and the loss of a job that she really loved. The job itself was not so important, of course — what really mattered was the separation from Bart, the fear that she might never see him again, the agony of loving that was denied even the small comfort of daily contact with him.

"Do you think I'm making too much

of it all?" she asked tentatively, offering him a lead, desperately hoping that some miracle might bring about a renewal of the former understanding and friendship.

He was swift to understand and equally swift to reject. It would be intolerable to have her about the office in close but distant contact, to have her near and know she was forbidden to him, to ache with loving and wanting and yet not even dare to touch her for fear of another rebuff. She had made it extremely clear that she wanted none of him, he thought grimly . . . a little light flirtation came easily and naturally to her and he had made the mistake of feeding that insatiable ego but at the first hint of real emotion she had abruptly withdrawn. She did not want his love or his lovemaking in earnest. She played an amusing game of love only so far as it suited her . . . and while she had obviously chosen to leap into bed with the man who had played a prominent part in her life of late, she was apparently not inclined to be so generous towards him, Bart thought with some bitterness.

"I want you to go," he said harshly. "One can't turn back the pages. I can never look at you and not remember . . . I haven't your light touch in these matters, I'm afraid."

"My light touch?" she echoed swiftly, a little puzzled, even indignant because of some implication in his tone. "What does that mean, exactly?"

He gestured impatiently. "It means that someone like Lucas Winfull or Rennie Bruce will adapt more readily to the way you play the game . . . I prefer the traditional rules. I'm sorry but I have no time for cheats." He heard the swift intake of her breath and turned to look at her with a faint smile. "Poor Georgina . . . you don't even realise that you cheat, do you? *Flirtation is fun and who gets hurt* . . . I've heard you say it, my dear. Who gets hurt? You do, Georgina — in the long run. It will be more than your fingers that sizzle one of these days!"

"In my experience, it's the men who cheat!" she threw at him furiously, eyes blazing, incensed that he should dare to dismiss her as a light-hearted flirt. She had won herself that reputation, she admitted . . . she had set out to keep to light flirtation and avoid all the pitfalls of loving — and it was a great pity that she had not stuck to her resolution!

They had almost reached the villa and she struck across the sand, leaving him, half-running with his jacket slipping from her shoulders until it fell in a tumbled heap to be ignored by her and picked up by Bart as he followed without haste . . .

11

IN the cold light of day, it all seemed to be such a mountain out of a molehill. She had walked with Bart in the moonlight, knowing that he wanted her as she wanted him, knowing that he did not and never would love her but anxious to snatch at a brief and precious happiness with him. She had embraced him and kissed him and murmured his name . . . and then so foolishly panicked because she had not realised that such passion could lie behind a cool, self-sufficient exterior. She had resisted and he had desisted . . . and if she really possessed the light touch that he had attributed to her then she would have known just how to soothe his hurt pride and smooth away the awkwardness of the moment. She had supposed that they were friends who liked and understood each other . . . but the incident proved that they were strangers still.

Because he was a stranger, albeit inexpressibly dear to her, she could not go to him and put things right. She did not know what she was going to do, in fact, but it was obvious that she could not remain at the villa. She had known herself to be an awkward third from the beginning — and now she wondered for the first time how Prudence would react if she knew that Bart and his secretary had come close to being lovers. Just now, she probably would not react at all . . . and Georgina could not help feeling that the other woman had forfeited her right to Bart's love and loyalty by her affair with John Jordan. But later she would want Bart again, Georgina thought shrewdly . . . when Prudence got over her present sadness she would turn again to Bart and be grateful for his love and no doubt they would be married, after all.

Prudence was so lucky in owning

a love that was willing to overlook the tempestuous affair that she had blazoned before the world without a thought for Bart's feelings, Georgina thought bleakly. Bart must love her very much to forgive so readily!

It was obvious that Prudence was suffering because of the tragic end to that affair and Georgina felt compassion for her. At the same time she felt that to have the man one loved snatched away by death might be preferable to losing him to someone else . . . and must be preferable to the lasting humiliation of rejection without reason such as she had known at Rennie's hands!

She toyed with the idea of having breakfast in her room but she had never been that kind of coward and so she went to face Bart with a composure that bravely concealed her sickness of heart. The table on the terrace was laid for breakfast but there was no sign of Bart. Not knowing whether to be glad or sorry, to hope that he would eventually appear or to dread his arrival, Georgina poured coffee for herself and broke a roll into tiny pieces without eating any of it . . . and tried not to recall the enchantment of the night when she had sat and talked and laughed with Bart at this very table in this very place. *Everything is spoiled*, she had said piteously . . . and it was so true. Nothing could ever be the same — and even the good memories were marred by the bad.

She decided that it would be sensible to take the first plane back to London and the *Elysium* and organise things so that Bart returned to find her replacement already installed and everything running smoothly. Evelyn was a pearl beyond price but she could not be expected to cope with all the work that must be piling up — and there was absolutely nothing to keep her in Mentone, Georgina told herself firmly.

Bart hesitated at sight of her, so cool and composed, glancing idly through a newspaper as though nothing had happened to affect her equanimity. He envied her ability to forget and dismiss. For himself, he was still sore and angry. In all his life, he had never loved as he loved Georgina . . . and he could not forgive her for mattering so much or himself for being such a fool. He was determined to conquer the way he felt about her — and equally determined that she should never know how he felt about her!

It was fortunate that she had pointed out the impossibility of continuing as his secretary. Her departure would leave a terrible void in his life but it must surely mean that he would get over her all the sooner. Daily contact, constant reminders, would be no help at all to a man with his complaint, he thought grimly . . . the only cure was to cut her out of his life for ever and completely. No man could go on loving without some encouragement, without some hope, so he must eventually cease to care for her, he told himself firmly.

Very much aware of his presence

although he was still and silent, Georgina put down the newspaper and reached for the coffee pot. "Good morning," she said quietly. "It's a lovely morning, isn't it? Shall I pour your coffee?"

Bart moved towards her, unsmiling. "Good morning," he responded, his tone softening even against his will. He seemed to be quite helpless in the face of her loveliness, her appeal, he told himself wryly . . . it cost him a great deal to sit down at the table without touching her. How easy, how naturally it would have been to rest his hand on her slim shoulder for a brief moment . . . and how desperately he needed the smallest of physical contacts to ease that ache within him.

Georgina did not recognise the quality of tenderness in his tone. The words seemed curt and perfunctory and he did not smile or lightly touch her hand with his own as he sat down although it would have cost him nothing, she thought bleakly, marvelling that he was so unaware of the dismay that wrapped itself so tightly about her heart.

They both took care that their hands should not touch as he took the cup of coffee from her and then accepted the newspaper from her hand with a little nod of thanks. Georgina watched him in silence as he drank his coffee and scanned the headlines and noticed that he did not make even the smallest pretence of eating. She said abruptly: "Bart, you don't need me here . . . I may as well go back to London if I can get a flight."

He glanced at her indifferently. "As you wish. I shall stay with Prudence until after the inquest, of course."

"You *don't* need me, do you?" she asked, desperately hoping that he would contradict the statement.

"No," he agreed without emotion.

She bit her lip to control its betraying quiver at the bleak reply. "Why did you want me with you at all?" she asked curiously.

He was surprised that she demanded explanation for the obvious. "If Prudence had been badly hurt then it would have been necessary for me to stay here for some time," he pointed out patiently. "As it turns out, I expect to be back in London by Tuesday or Wednesday . . . but I daresay you are anxious to get back to your own affairs. It was good of you to come with me at such short notice," he added stiffly. "I doubt if your young man approved."

She frowned. "Do you mean Mathew . . . ?"

"If that's his name," he said indifferently.

"He isn't my young man — whatever the phrase might imply," she said slowly. "We are cousins — and he flew off to foreign parts himself yesterday . . . to South Africa, in fact."

Bart was wholly disinterested as to the man's movements but he was surprised that she should claim him as a cousin. It was the first mention of a family relationship, he thought drily.

Perhaps they were cousins but that was no bar to another kind of relationship, he decided grimly, remembering that she had been obviously discomfited by his unexpected arrival at her flat in the early morning. Dismay, guilt and embarrassment had been written all over her pretty face, he thought angrily . . .

"I doubt if you'll even miss him," he said, deliberately offensive. "Off with the old and on with the new is your motto, isn't it? Now I understand why you gave me so much encouragement . . . I'm sorry I couldn't play it your way for it might have been very rewarding in the end. But you'll soon find someone else, you know."

Angry colour swept into her face. Quite involuntarily, she raised her hand and slapped the mocking little smile from his handsome face. Abruptly his eyes hardened and his mouth tightened and a nerve throbbed in the lean cheek that bore the imprint of her fingers. Instinctively he caught her by the slender wrist and his grip bruised the soft flesh before he released her, almost contemptuously.

"We'll forget that happened," he said coldly.

She rubbed her bruised wrist . . . and looked with regret at the marks of her fingers on his face. "It shouldn't have happened . . . but you mustn't speak to me like that, Bart. You meant to insult me," she said slowly, wondering.

He rose to his feet. "I'll take you to the airport as soon as you are ready. I expect we can get you a seat on one of the flights."

He was dismissing the entire incident and indignation rose within her for she was entitled to some explanation of his offensive words. But one look at his set face told her that he would not offer her any explanation . . . and she could not force one from him. "Rennie Bruce will be here shortly," she said in a hard little voice that did not betray the throbbing regret she felt. "We are supposed to be spending the day together and I'm sure he will drive me to the airport. So I need not put you to any trouble."

He looked down at her in astonishment. "You don't miss the smallest opportunity, do you?" he demanded harshly. "When did you arrange to have the day with Bruce . . . this morning?"

"Yesterday . . . if it's any of your business!" she retorted, her chin tilting before the contempt in his eyes. What did it matter what he thought of her — or that he construed her friendship with every other man in the wrong way? Let him suppose that Mathew was more lover than cousin! Let him imagine her fickle and inconstant and ready to let any man make love to her! If he was so ready to think so badly of her then his good opinion was not worth the having!

"You're incredible," he said slowly, baffled by her behaviour.

Georgina shrugged. "Rennie and I are old friends . . . I told you!" she said lightly and her tone implied that the relationship had gone far beyond that of mere friendship.

He turned away from the defiance in her eyes. It was not his business, as she had pointed out . . . but he failed to understand the nature of a girl who could be dancing on cloud number seven for days because of one man's meaningful attentions, cousin or no cousin: could dismiss him with a light heart as soon as he went away and offer obvious encouragement to Rennie Bruce when circumstances brought him back into her life; and could then push him to the back of her mind to give a convincing display of warm delight in another man's attentions, melting into his arms and raising her face to be kissed as though he were the only man in the world that mattered. That, of course, was the secret of Georgina's magic, he thought wryly. She had the gift of making a man feel that he was the one and only in her life — and the odd thing was that briefly each man *was* the one and only! Such was the fickleness and inconstancy and worthlessness of a heart that no man could really want to possess, he decided grimly . . . and turned away, determined that he would not go on loving such a woman!

"I'll say goodbye, then," Georgina said, a little desperately.

He paused to look back. "Goodbye, Georgina."

Formal, cold, unforgiving . . . his tone struck at the innermost sensitivity of her being. "We probably won't see each other again," she said stiffly, forcing back the tears.

His heart seized in the brutal grip of dismay at the light, careless tone. "There isn't any point, don't you agree," he returned indifferently, resolutely resisting the nudge of instinct that urged him to go to her, take her into his arms, kiss away the foolishness and the coldness that was turning them into strangers who did not even like each other.

"No . . . well . . . " she swallowed the ache of tears in her throat. "Goodbye, Bart . . . " Pride came to her rescue and her words were uttered lightly as though it did not matter that her heart was slowly being torn into tiny pieces.

"Safe journey," he said lightly . . . and if he had only smiled with the words, held out his hand, she would have flown into his arms and begged for forgiveness and cried out her love and her need. But he did not smile and he went away without making the slightest move towards her — and they were spared her betrayal and his embarrassment. Georgina sat very still amid the clutter of breakfast things, her hands clenched so tightly that her nails dug angry crescents into the soft palms . . . and her pain was much too great for the easy balm of tears, after all.

When Rennie came, she was smiling and eager and bright-eyed and he could not be blamed for supposing that she was as anxious as he was to forget all the unhappiness and remember only the delight of the past.

She allowed him to believe that she was going back to London at Bart's suggestion because she was needed at the *Elysium* . . . and was surprised when he promptly suggested that they should travel together. For things were at a standstill on the set and it now seemed probable that the film would never be finished. It had been Jordan's 'baby' from the beginning and with his tragic death no one seemed to know what was going to happen. Filming had ceased for the moment, anyway — and there was no reason why Rennie should stay in Mentone if Georgina was going to be in London!

She was almost glad of his company. He was confident and demanding and allowed her very little opportunity to dwell on all that had happened between herself and Bart. All that had happened, she echoed wryly . . . so little had happened and yet sufficient to destroy her peace of mind and all her happiness.

They were in London to enjoy a late lunch at a little restaurant that had been one of their favourite haunts in earlier days. Rennie seemed to be trying desperately to recreate the atmosphere of the time when she had supposed herself to be very much in love and he had been set on seducing her although she had been too naïve to realise the truth. Now the tables were turned, in a way, she thought drily . . . for he had convinced himself that he cared for her and she was preparing to use him in a cold, calculating way as a camouflage for the heartache and humiliation she was suffering because of Bart Blair. And Rennie played into her hands all unconsciously . . .

He took her back to the little flat after the meal . . . and seemed reluctant to leave her. Georgina could not summon sufficient interest to send him away and so he stayed while she unpacked and tidied and dusted with a becoming air of domesticity that delighted him.

At last, as she passed the sofa where

he lounged, he reached for her and drew her down and kissed her, gently, without passion. She was passive rather than responsive, submissive rather than encouraging, and he felt a stirring of dismay. He had been patient, feeling his way, anxious not to alarm or displease or awaken any reminders that might damage his chances now that he knew how very important she was to him. She had been warm and friendly, filling him with hope, even confidence . . . but now she lay in his arms and seemed scarcely aware of the touch of his lips with their careful lack of urgency.

"Still hating me, Gina?" he asked ruefully.

Something in his tone caught at her generous heart. She touched her hand to his cheek in a gesture that was peculiarly her own. "I never thought of hating you," she said truthfully.

"Did you miss me at all?"

"Very much," she told him honestly. "You were very important to me, Rennie." Not as important as she

213

had supposed but important all the same and he was not easily dismissed from her life. Her feeling for him had been the forerunner to real loving, after all. If she had never thought she loved Rennie, she might never have realised that her feeling for Bart was real and lasting and all-consuming love. "I was . . . very fond of you," she added, nostalgically, almost wishing she could recapture the days when Bart Blair had been just a name to her.

"You loved me, Gina," he said quietly. "I took it for granted then . . . bloody fool!" He traced the lovely lines of her face with gentle, caressing fingers. "Lovely Gina, you knew we belonged together but I was too blind to see and too stubborn to want to know. Now — Gina, I want you so much! I want you to marry me . . . soon!"

Her heart was thudding so heavily that she felt sick. It was ironic that he should utter the words that she had once ached to hear . . . and that they should be so empty and meaningless now. "You can't be serious," she said slowly. "You can't mean it." She scarcely knew if she wanted him to be in earnest or if she wanted him to go away and never trouble her again.

Rennie did not move or speak for a moment. Then he drew a gold ring from the little finger of his right hand . . . a ring that he always wore and valued highly as a gift from his mother. He took her left hand firmly and pushed the ring over the knuckle of the third finger. "Does that convince you?" he asked quietly.

Georgina stared at the band on her finger — and felt nothing. No warm delight, no glow of happiness, no thankfulness at a dream come true as she might have known such a short time before. It was too late and she no longer believed that she loved him or that he could make her happy. Yet she did not slip the ring from her finger . . . let it stay for it did not matter if she married Rennie or any other man as she could never have the one man she truly loved and wanted.

"Yes, I'm convinced," she said slowly.

For there was nothing he could have said or done to convince her so completely of his sincerity. That simple transference of a ring from his hand to her own carried more weight than all the wordy declarations, all the passionate demonstrations, in the world . . .

12

"I'M engaged!" Georgina announced brightly. "I'm getting married!"

Already she had told a couple of neighbours, the paper-seller on the corner, the friendly policeman at the crossroad, the front-of-the-house manager and the cashier, Bryan King and one of the electricians, the stage-doorkeeper and half the members of the company — and she would not listen to the insistence of her heart that it was all bravado. She refused to doubt the wisdom of marrying a man she did not love and did not really trust — and she chose to ignore the apprehension that kept tugging at her heart.

She had always loved Rennie and nothing had really changed, she told herself stubbornly . . . that foolish feeling for Bart Blair was merely infatuation, a passing fancy. Lonely and

217

depressed, she had allowed herself to be enchanted by the physical magnetism of a very attractive man.

Evelyn exclaimed and congratulated and asked all the right questions without showing her instinctive dismay and disappointment. From the beginning, she had felt that Georgina would do very well for Bart . . . and it was quite time that he married. She was a nice girl, warm and generous and sweet, wholly endearing — and she would bring new meaning to his rather bleak life. She was Richard Durrell's daughter and that endeared her to Evelyn who had known the actor years before. But sentiment apart, Georgina had been steeped in the atmosphere and lore of the theatre since infancy and so she knew and loved and understood the world that meant so much to Bart Blair.

Evelyn was convinced that they were right for each other. It did not mean much that Bart had always treated the girl with business-like impersonality or that Georgina had light-heartedly tripped through life in the company of one man after another . . . or that one would need to be an incurable romantic to visualise them as man and wife. Evelyn *was* incurably romantic and she had felt that love was quietly and steadily growing between them and would show itself when the time was ripe.

Prudence had been the only stumbling-block but she had met and fallen headlong in love with someone else and then it had seemed to Evelyn that Bart might feel sufficiently freed from the restrictions of that affair to look around him and notice his pretty secretary.

But John Jordan had died and Bart had flown to France to be with Prudence like the good, reliable friend that he was . . . and the only fuel for Evelyn's little dream was that unexpected decision to take Georgina with him. It seemed to her that Bart might have seized an opportunity to get to know the girl outside the obvious confines of the office.

Evelyn knew that she was a romantic old fool but she firmly believed in destiny . . . and it seemed to her that Georgina was flying in the face of her destiny with her promise to marry another man. She wondered what had happened in Mentone to bring Georgina back to London so soon and hurl her into a foolish engagement. Georgina might declare that she had known Rennie Bruce at RADA and expected to marry him and broken with him through a foolish misunderstanding and no doubt it was true but Evelyn did not think that the girl was still in love with the actor. She was too animated, too talkative, too elated — and Evelyn knew that real happiness did not express itself so easily. One was too full for words and scarcely dared to mention one's happiness for fear it vanished at a touch. It would be much more convincing if even a natural extrovert like Georgina retreated into her quiet world of dreams at this time.

Instead she went about telling everyone, waving Rennie's ring like a talisman as she declared her good fortune . . . and within a day or two the whole of theatreland had heard of the engagement. It even reached the gossip columns of the newspapers . . . partly because she was a Durrell and that famous family was always news and partly because of Rennie's connection with the film that had been so abruptly abandoned.

Georgina would not allow Rennie to replace the gold ring with a more conventional engagement ring and she did not pause to ask herself if she really meant to allow him to replace it with a wedding ring in due course. For the moment she was merely thankful for the boost to her ego that their engagement had provided. It was a much-needed boost for her confidence had been at a very low ebb . . . it was very comforting to be loved and wanted and urged into marriage just when another man was so heartbreakingly indifferent.

Rennie had changed. He was no longer conceited and arrogant, irritatingly sure of himself, taking without any thought of giving. He loved her and love brought humility and self-doubt together with the anxious fear that he might not be good enough for the girl who had promised to marry him . . . and he set out to please in every way. He was tender and loving, gentle and undemanding and very patient with her moods. He wanted an early wedding naturally. Georgina knew there was no point in delay for the miracle was simply not going to happen . . . Bart did not feel anything for her and would not make the smallest move to prevent her marriage to another man. Yet she would not commit herself to a definite date, declaring lightly that she wanted to enjoy being a fiancée for a little longer as she would be a wife for the rest of her life. And Rennie accepted because he might so easily lose her if he protested . . .

She used her engagement as the excuse for leaving the *Elysium*, allowing everyone to suppose that she would be married very soon and needed all her time for wedding preparations and the buying of a trousseau. Determined and efficient, she cleared as much of the office work as possible and arranged for a temporary secretary to take over from her. When Bart telephoned to say that he would be back on Wednesday she immediately decided to be gone before he arrived at the theatre. It was painful talking to him . . . it would be even more painful to meet him again, she thought bleakly. She had meant to tell him of her engagement but the words froze on her lips . . . instead she blurted out all the arrangements she had made for her imminent departure from his employment.

Bart missed her very much and knew that nothing could change the way he felt about her. Loving Georgina was as inevitable as breathing . . . no matter what she was or what she did, he could not love her less. Impatient with the circumstances that kept him from her, quite determined on a better understanding between them in the future, he was thankful when he could arrange the return to England. He telephoned to tell Georgina of his plans, hoping that she might sound just a little glad of his return, meaning to pave the way to a renewal of friendship with a few, well-chosen words . . . and found her cold, unfriendly, wholly indifferent and obviously determined to leave the *Elysium* as soon as possible.

He said levelly and without emotion: "Yes, I understand . . . yes, that's all right. I take it the new girl is fairly efficient and knows something about theatre work? Good . . . !"

He replaced the receiver and sat for a while, staring blankly at the instrument. Georgina was proud and stubborn . . . having declared her intention to leave him she was determined to go through with it, he thought wryly. Well, that did not matter. He did not want her for a secretary any more, anyway . . . it was much too restricting. He desperately wanted to marry her, to have her with him for always, to love her and cherish her and look after her to the best of his ability. There seemed to be very little point in a way of life that did not include Georgina . . . and he had even lost interest in his beloved theatre for what incentive did a man have for success if he had no real happiness or peace of mind in his personal life? With Georgina by his side, he could conquer the world! Without her, he would not care if he lost the *Elysium* to one of the big combines!

Prudence came into the room but he was not immediately aware of her and she looked at him, wondering at his preoccupation with thoughts that did not seem to bring him much pleasure. Something was very wrong, she knew . . . but he would not confide in her because he felt that his problems must seem trivial in comparison with her grief. It was impossible to make him understand that she was not grieving for Jordan who would expect her to make a new life without him. Their happiness had been so short-lived that it all seemed like a dream — one that would never fade or be forgotten but held less and less reality as the days passed.

She laid her hand on Bart's shoulder. "What is it? I wish you'd tell me," she said lightly.

Swiftly he covered her hand with his own and smiled. "Nothing that need concern you," he said carelessly. "I'm losing my secretary, that's all."

Prudence was not deceived by the seeming indifference of his tone. For there was a bleakness in his smile and it did not reach his eyes. "Oh . . . ?" she said slowly. "That's sudden, isn't it? I thought she was so happy at the *Elysium*. Why is she leaving, Bart?"

He hesitated. Then he said steadily: "Oh, personal reasons." He busied himself with lighting a cigarette, avoiding her too-perceptive eyes.

"You'll miss her," Prudence said quietly.

"Yes, indeed . . . I'm sorry to lose her," he returned brightly. "She's a nice girl and we got on well together."

"Until you brought her here," Prudence commented shrewdly. "I'm not prying, Bart . . . and heaven forbid that you should imagine I'm jealous. But I wasn't so wrapped up in myself that I couldn't see how things were with you and Georgina."

He looked at her quickly, eyes narrowing. "And how were things, Prudence? You must have seen something that I didn't!" he exclaimed drily.

She smiled. "Bart, I'm not an absolute idiot and I've been telling you for months that you've a soft spot for Georgina! And she's very fond of you!"

"Absurd!" he exclaimed.

"Not so absurd," she returned firmly.

"She was always on the defensive with me . . . afraid I'd sense the way she felt and resent it, perhaps. She never liked me very much . . . which would be very natural if she fancied you, wouldn't it?"

A wry smile tugged at his lips. "It might be convincing if Georgina didn't fancy so many men," he said drily. "She's a butterfly by nature."

"People are not always what they seem," Prudence pointed out quietly. "Flirting can be a search for love — or a defence against loving. Perhaps Georgina was determined not to be hurt . . . and perhaps she had her reasons. Who knows? Do *you* know? She's a very out-going person and yet she doesn't really tell people much about herself, does she? She's proud and sensitive and really rather shy, I imagine . . . and you'll be very stupid if you let her slip through your fingers, Bart! Because you're in love with her, aren't you?"

He was silent for a moment. Then

he said wryly: "So much in love that I'm tempted to believe you are right . . . and that could be disastrous! For I've no proof at all that Georgina finds me at all attractive . . . and she seems to have slipped through my fingers already!"

"Don't be a defeatist!" she admonished him. "Faint heart thoroughly deserves to lose fair lady, you know . . . !"

Miles away, across the channel from France, Georgina sat at her desk, staring at the silent telephone with Bart's cold and unemotional words echoing in her ears. There had not been a single word or one slight cadence that she could construe as regret that she was going . . . and it did not occur to her that his pride might be as great as her own. After all, Bart had never really cared anything about her . . . all these months he had treated her with brisk impersonality and regarded her as nothing more than an intelligent and efficient member of his staff. That brief episode in Mentone was not even worth remembering, she thought bleakly . . . and knew it was etched on her heart and mind for ever.

The next morning she was a little pale but composed as she ensured that everything was in perfect order in readiness for Bart's return and then went about the theatre making her farewells. Everyone was sorry to see her go and she was touched by their expressions of affection and goodwill and troubled by the little gifts that were pressed upon her for her 'bottom drawer'. She felt that she was flying under false colours and yet it seemed probable that she would marry Rennie in the end. She was drifting towards that particular harbour on a sea of apathy . . .

Stuart carelessly wished her happy and was obviously unaffected by her marriage plans although it was only a short time since he had declared himself in love with her. Georgina smiled a little wryly for his indifference smote her with the reminder of how little she really meant to everyone but Rennie . . . and she was not so sure that *his* renewed love would last.

The tide appeared to have turned for *Devil's Delight* for the critics had paid a second visit and given it grudging approval. Stuart had been stimulated into attempting a successor and so he had been too preoccupied to take much interest in her engagement. Now he said suddenly: "It doesn't bother you . . . what they say about marriage between cousins? I wouldn't care for it myself."

She stared. "You've got it wrong," she said lightly. "I'm not marrying my cousin."

"Oh . . . ? Not marrying Mathew!" he exclaimed in surprise. "Why not? You were living in his pocket all last week!"

She laughed. "A lot can happen in a week," she said airily. "I'm going to marry Rennie Bruce . . . and I never had the least intention of marrying Mathew!"

"Well, I'm amazed," he declared with obvious truth. "I thought you were madly in love with the fellow! Isn't that why you gave me the cold shoulder — and why Bart was so bloody to everyone last week?"

"Bart . . .!" she exclaimed, her heart almost stopping at the implication of the words. "Why should it matter to him?"

He cast his eyes to heaven. "The girl's blind!" he announced to no one in particular.

"Don't be silly," Georgina said slowly. "I don't mean a thing to Bart Blair . . . and he certainly didn't suppose or care that I loved Mathew!"

He shrugged. "All right, sweetie . . . have it your own way! But onlookers see more of the game than the participants . . . and I'm telling you that the way you appeared to feel about your good-looking cousin knocked Sir Bartholomew Blair for six!"

"But I didn't feel anything for Mathew! We're friends . . . cousins!"

she protested incredulously.

"Then perhaps you should have made it clear," Stuart suggested drily. "You might even have told me the facts of the matter and saved me a little heartache."

She caught his arm. "Oh, Stuart — I'm sorry! I didn't mean to hurt you . . . you know that! But you don't really care for me . . . not really!"

"If you say so," he said wryly.

"Bart doesn't care for me either," she said, her tone betraying that she hoped with all her heart that she was mistaken.

Stuart looked at her steadily. Then he smiled in sudden perception. "If you say so," he said lightly. "You know what you want, I daresay . . . if only for a few days at a time!"

A little smile tugged at her lips at the gentle teasing . . . a rueful little smile. "It does seem a bit like that, doesn't it?" she agreed, not minding that the whole world knew of her love for Bart Blair — as long as *he* did not! "I know what I want," she added quietly. "But I don't imagine getting it!"

"That's the trouble with women . . . no imagination," Stuart drawled. He put an arm about her and kissed her cheek. "My dear girl, if you know what you want why not make some effort to get it," he suggested. "Don't settle for second-best!"

It was good advice . . . but she could not follow it. For she could not trust his intuition where Bart's feelings were concerned . . . and her own instincts seemed to be very unreliable! She wondered that anyone could have regarded her enjoyment of Mathew's brief visit as a sign of loving but, looking back, she remembered how readily she had given her time to him, how openly she had delighted in his affection and interest and company. She was fond of Mathew and the Durrells were strong on family ties. But it was all so innocent that it had not occurred to her that anyone could misconstrue their relationship. But if so, then it must have been just as easy for Stuart to misconstrue Bart's brusqueness and bad temper that had certainly been born of the affair *á la* Prudence and John Jordan rather than her behaviour!

It would be madness to suppose that Bart cared how many men flitted in and out of her life . . . although he *had* criticised her for flirting and warned her that she would be badly burned if she continued to play with fire! Why should he care? How was it possible that he cared? Oh God . . . if only he *did* care!

Of course she had flirted . . . deliberately, desperately, defensively throwing herself at the head of any man who gave her a second glance . . . every man in fact but the one she wanted with all her heart. She had kept him at a distance because she might love him too much . . . and so it had proved. She had not played with the fire that was Bart Blair but she had been badly burned just the same. Her heart would carry the scar for the rest of time . . .

13

GEORGINA went from the small and much-loved theatre with an ache in her throat for all the good times she had known within its walls and for the circumstances which forced her to leave it when she wanted so much to stay.

She left by the stage door . . . just as Bart arrived at the front of the theatre, pushing his way into the foyer and wasting little time on pleasantries with the staff before mounting the stairs to the office three at a time, his heart pounding with impatience.

A stranger sat at Georgina's desk. A neat, slender wide-eyed stranger with a shining cap of dark hair and a slightly nervous smile for him as he entered. Bart scarcely looked at her. He walked into his own office and then returned to look about the outer office as though he suspected Georgina to be hiding behind a filing cabinet or under a desk.

"Can I help you?" Jessica Wise asked, trying to sound efficient.

"Where's Georgina?" he demanded without ceremony.

Her eyes widened a little at his tone. She had worked for a theatrical agent and was used to the volatile behaviour of those connected with the theatre but she decided that she did *not* like this thoroughly rude and bad-tempered man. He was glowering at her in a positive fury. "I'm afraid she doesn't work here any more," she said brightly, soothingly. "Can I help you at all, Mr . . . ?"

"I'm Bart Blair," he told her impatiently and turned thankfully to Evelyn as she entered, dear and familiar and reassuring. "Georgina . . . !" he demanded. "Where is she?"

"Oh dear," Evelyn said, a little dismayed. "Has she left already? That's rather naughty when she must have known that you would want to see her!

And you're earlier than we expected, Bart."

"Yes . . . I nearly killed myself to get here before two o'clock," he said drily. "I had a feeling that Georgina meant to slip away without seeing me!"

Aware of the steadily-widening and very interested gaze of the girl at the desk, Evelyn laid a gentle, warning hand on his arm. "I expect she's just slipped out for something, dear. She's a very polite child and she wouldn't dream of leaving without making her farewells in proper fashion. Come and sit down and I'll pour you a drink. I expect you want something after your journey. Jessica, I think you might go now although it isn't quite two . . . be back by five, won't you?" She drew Bart into the inner office, saying quietly so that only he could hear: "She's a nice girl, very willing — but one can't rely on the discretion of strangers, you know."

Bart smiled wryly. He dropped into a chair with the sudden weariness of someone who has been taut with anticipation only to meet with disappointment. Seeing the look in his eyes, Evelyn knew that he did care for Georgina . . . but there was no satisfaction in being proved right, after all. Again she wondered what had happened in Mentone to force Georgina into a most unsuitable engagement and to bring that particular look into his dark eyes.

"She really did it," he said heavily. "I kept hoping she would change her mind, you know . . . even though I know that she's proud and stubborn and quite determined to have her own way."

Evelyn thought he referred to her decision to marry Rennie Bruce. She said gently: "I expect she's very fond of him, dear . . . and she's known him some time, hasn't she? Perhaps she'll be happy now . . . and I did tell you that there was something on her mind, do you remember?"

Bart looked at her in bewilderment.

"What do you mean? What are you talking about?" He frowned. "What did Georgina tell you, for heaven's sake!"

"Oh, she told me what she told everyone else," Evelyn said slowly.

"Yes . . . ?" Bart queried impatiently. "What was that?"

"That she was getting married very soon," Evelyn said carefully, suddenly realising that he had not known when she saw the tautening of his expression and the little movement, quite involuntary, that spilled the brandy from his glass. "She didn't tell you?" Her tone was deliberately casual for he was proud and very sensitive and would not wish her to know how much pain she inflicted with the announcement.

"No, she didn't tell me," he said slowly. He leaned back in his chair, closing his eyes . . . and a nerve throbbed in his cheek like a wild thing. "Who's the lucky man? There are so many men in Georgina's life that I don't care to hazard a guess."

"Why, it's the actor — Rennie Bruce," Evelyn said lightly. "I gather they met when they were both at RADA and that there was some silly quarrel."

"*Rennie Bruce!*" he echoed incredulously. He stared at her, shocked and dismayed . . . and absolutely refuting the very thought. Quite inexplicably, his heart lightened and a little smile began to play about his lips. If it had been any other man he might have believed that Georgina was wholly lost to him. But she would never marry a man like Bruce! Her sudden and bewildering engagement could only be an act of defiance, conscious or otherwise! Bart was suddenly convinced that pride had pushed her into the other man's arms . . . pride and a determination to punish him for his stupidity! She had far too much sense to marry the man, of course! He said drily: "It sounds like a fairy story to me, Evelyn. Bruce is too ambitious . . . if he marries at all it will be

241

someone who can give him a helping hand on the way to fame and fortune."

"I don't know about that, dear. But Georgina wears a ring that he gave her — and their engagement has been in all the newspapers," Evelyn said quietly. "She has been telling everyone of her plans to marry him, Bart." She understood his natural reluctance to accept but there was no point in refusing to face facts.

"Expecting the news to reach me rather sooner than it did, I suspect," he said with a dry smile. "But I haven't looked at an English paper in days."

Evelyn did not ask why Georgina should want him to learn of her engagement by such a devious route. Perhaps he had good reason to know that she would not tell him herself, she thought shrewdly. She said lightly: "You must be the only person she didn't tell!"

"Because I'd ask too many questions and she wouldn't have the answers," he returned promptly. "And that's why she wouldn't wait to face me today. She hasn't the slightest intention of marrying Bruce . . . and she must know that I shall say as much when I see her! She has far too much sense, Evelyn."

She understood that he was desperately trying to convince himself. "A girl in love isn't always very sensible," she said gently.

Bart knew a sudden vision of a girl with a great deal of sweetness in her smile and shy candour in her eyes as she leaned to bestow a kiss with swift and generous and surely loving warmth. He knew a sudden realisation that he had misunderstood Georgina from the beginning, thinking her a heartless flirt who took without giving when she had merely been a girl looking for love in all the wrong places. He knew a sudden conviction that she had found what she sought in him and offered a loving heart in exchange. He had drawn back, misunderstanding and mistrusting that precious gift. He had supposed her to be flirting with the lightness of heart he had always condemned. He had supposed her to be merely playing at love and he had been too hurt and disappointed and angry to realise that she did not offer him rainbow gold but the warm reality of lasting love . . .

"That's true," Bart said slowly, carefully. "Getting herself engaged to the wrong man is just the sort of nonsensical thing a girl in love might do!" And he laughed softly, indulgently and with a great deal of warm tenderness in the sound. "I'm afraid that love makes fools of us all, Evelyn," he added ruefully. "But it would be a dull old world without it!"

"You won't let her marry Rennie Bruce, will you?" Evelyn asked, a little anxiously, for men were strange, proud creatures and had been known to sacrifice their own happiness rather than admit to a very real need for the one woman who could provide it.

Bart smiled reassuringly. "No, I

won't let her marry him," he said firmly. "Georgina is going to marry me!"

His voice rang with confidence but he really did not know how he was going to work the miracle. It was all very well to be so sure that Georgina loved him — but she was wearing another man's ring and it might not be easy to persuade her to break her word. Perhaps persuasion was not the answer when so much depended on results. Perhaps *fait accompli* was more to the point . . .

The happy bride to be had never been so miserable in all her life. For Bart was not making the slightest attempt to get in touch with her. He was certainly back in London and so was Prudence Carroll and no doubt he was a very busy man between the demands of his theatre and the demands of the woman he loved. Much too busy to give her a second thought, Georgina decided wryly.

She had not expected to see or hear from him, of course. Yet she had hoped against hope. She did not really know what she had thought might happen . . . except perhaps that the overwhelming love within her might have found some small echo in his being and made it impossible for him to dismiss her so completely from his life.

It was intolerable to love him so much when there was not the slightest chance of being loved in return. It was impossible to look forward to a future without the only man in the world who matters. It was painful to think of marrying someone else when all her loving belonged to Bart . . . and yet Rennie talked of their coming marriage and she did not discourage or disillusion him and sometimes it was just as though Bart did not even exist, she thought unhappily.

Perhaps it *had* all been a dream, a figment of her imagination. Perhaps she had never worked for Bart Blair and learned to love him and gone with him to the South of France only to know the nearness and the dearness of him which had created such a tumult of wanting that she had almost betrayed how much she loved him. And that ache of love in her lonely, discouraged heart was so insistent that she knew it was no dream but painful reality. For it was not really wise to love as she loved Bart. It was better to be loved rather than the loving, she decided defensively: it was better to have a troubled conscience than a troubled heart, she decided defiantly — and allowed Rennie to go on believing that she would marry him.

As she would, of course, she told herself bleakly. For there didn't seem to be anything else to do and at least he would be happy. Bart would marry the beautiful Prudence and *they* would be happy. So it was only herself who might live with a heart that could not forget. For if she lived to be a hundred, Bart would still be in her heart and mind and blood . . . as dear to her then as now!

Georgina wandered about her little flat, bored and lonely and very unhappy. The days threatened to drag without the interest and entertainment of her job at the *Elysium*. For the time being she was inclined to avoid the friends who expected her to enthuse about wedding plans . . . after all, she was so uncertain of the future that she had not even told her family that she was engaged to Rennie Bruce. Her mother was in America on a lecture tour and obviously had not heard or she would have telephoned. She was also inclined to avoid the places that might involve her in even the briefest of encounters with Bart Blair and so she was reluctant to even shop in the neighbourhood for the *Elysium* was only a stone's throw from her flat.

Rennie had been suddenly offered a part in a play that was to be produced at the *Sphinx* . . . a leading rôle in a controversial play that might well make or break his career as an actor. She did not expect to see him that day as he would be caught up in discussions with producer and agent and fellow members of the cast. He was thrilled and delighted by the offer that had come out of the blue . . . due, he felt, to the publicity that he had received because of the abandoned film.

The telephone shrilled. Georgina picked up the receiver, half-expecting to hear Rennie's voice. But it was Jessica Wise, the friend who had taken her place at the *Elysium*.

"Message for you from the great Sir Bart," Jessica said gaily. "He's calling for you at twelve . . . please be ready to leave immediately as parking will be impossible. He'll pause by the main archway to pick you up."

Georgina was dumbfounded. "Calling for *me* . . . ?" she echoed.

"At twelve," Jessica confirmed. "Please be ready . . . I gather that's most important."

"Just like that," Georgina said slowly, bewildered.

"It does sound a bit peremptory," Jessica agreed. "But you warned me that he isn't the world's most courteous man!"

"How are you getting on with him?" Georgina asked impulsively.

"He frightens me to death," Jessica said in a tone that belied the words. "No . . . he's very nice, actually. Breaking me in gently, I suspect. How are *you*, Gee? I bet you love being a lady of leisure!"

"It's great," Georgina said drily. "Jessica, there's some mistake, you know . . . Bart and I haven't any arrangement to meet today."

"I may not be the Secretary of the Year but I can read my own shorthand," Jessica returned blithely. "It's no mistake. My boss was very definite. He's going out of town for a few days so perhaps he needs to see you about something urgent before he goes . . . and I bet he gives you lunch, lucky girl! Enjoy yourself and tell me all about it another time! Bye . . . !"

Georgina put down the telephone, her heart pounding with shock and bewilderment. She could not imagine what Bart wanted with her but there was urgency in that peremptory message and it was not like him to be quite so cavalier without good reason. But she could not think of anything important concerning him that could possibly concern her, too . . . and her heart leaped at the unexpected answer to all her prayers.

One glance at the clock and she fled to run a bath and then rummage through her wardrobe in the despairing conviction that she did not have a thing to wear! Was Bart going to give her lunch? Or were they going back to the theatre for some reason? If only she knew what it was all about! Heavens, what should she wear! She settled for a trouser suit, light grey and fashionably cut, with a charcoal grey shirt. Then she dashed back to the bathroom to hurtle half the contents of a jar of bath salts into the steaming water and herself after it, convinced that she would never be ready in time and wondering what possessed Bart to give her so little notice.

At two minutes to twelve, she was ready and giving herself a last, anxious scrutiny in the long mirror. She locked the door of the little flat behind her and hurried across the courtyard to the main archway that led out to the busy thoroughfare . . . and her eager, throbbing heart almost stopped at sight of the familiar white Rolls-Royce drawing into the kerb.

Bart, tall and very handsome and unsmiling, got out of the car and came round to open the passenger door. "Georgina . . . " he said formally, in greeting.

She looked up at him, a little breathless, so glad to see him that she could not even speak his name. Without a word, she got into the car and he closed the door and went round to the driving seat, ignoring the noisy, indignant klaxons of the traffic that the big car blocked in that narrow but extremely busy road.

Bart put the car into gear and they moved away, gliding easily with the stream of traffic. He did not look at her or say anything, concentrating solely on driving the big car. Georgina stole a glance at him, her hands clenched tightly on the grey velvet bag in her lap. Bart manoeuvred the car in and out of buses and taxis and delivery vans. They left the section of London that is known as Theatreland via Charing Cross Road, rounded Trafalgar Square and turned into Whitehall, drove straight across at Parliament Square and passed the Palace of Westminster and headed along the Embankment . . . and all in silence.

There was something oddly reassuring about that silence, Georgina discovered . . . it was just as though they shared an affinity that did not need words. Suddenly there was no need for explanation of that peremptory message or his unexpected desire to see her or even his failure to tell her what it was all about. Suddenly she was at ease and she relaxed the nervous grip on her bag and settled more comfortably into her seat and looked about her with interest as they crossed Lambeth Bridge towards the south side of the river.

That painful, apprehensive excitement within her began to subside and a quiet little glow of content seemed to be taking its place. For she was with Bart and that was all that really mattered. She was with him in his car, sitting beside him, going she knew not where but content to be with him, content to trust him, content to leave everything to his capable management. She had no idea what was in his mind but when he was ready to do so, he would tell her what it was all about, she decided confidently.

At that point, Bart turned his head to look at her. He smiled . . . and there was something almost boyish and certainly mischievous in that smile. She raised an amused eyebrow.

"I'm kidnapping you, Georgina," he said lightly. "Do you mind . . . ?"

14

GEORGINA laughed, not believing him. How could she believe him! It was too ridiculous! No man could or would kidnap a girl in broad daylight without good reason . . . and Bart had no need to kidnap her when she would willingly go to the ends of the earth with him at a word.

"Oh, I don't mind," she said lightly, entering into the spirit of the thing. "Anything that pleases you, Bart. But why?"

He had known as soon as she looked up at him with that certain glow in her eyes that all would be well, that he had not mistaken the way she felt about him, that he had not made the biggest blunder of his life with his careful, determined planning of recent days . . . and he knew now as he met her dancing eyes that she was and always would be the only woman for him. She was sheer delight with her swift and perceptive understanding, her quick and intelligent wit, her delicious sense of humour that so well matched his own.

He said evenly: "It seemed so much easier than making explanations all round."

Something in his tone caused her to look at him swiftly, startled, wondering if she had been too ready to laugh at those outrageous words. "Bart, you're joking!" she declared optimistically.

"No, I'm not," he said decisively. "I never joke about serious things . . . and I'm very serious about you." He took a hand from the wheel and covered the slim hands that were again gripping her bag for dear life. "Relax, Georgina," he said lightly, reassuringly. "My intentions are perfectly honourable, I promise. I have a special licence in my pocket and we are going to be married in Hurstmonceux at four o'clock. I must say your mother has been marvellous," he went on admiringly. "I left all the arrangements at that end to her and she seems to have moved mountains!"

Georgina was very pale. She stared at him as though she could not believe her ears. "You're quite mad," she said slowly, incredulously.

He laughed. "I expect so . . . but I find that I can't live without you, Georgina. Can you live without me? No, don't answer because I'm not giving you a choice!"

"Of all the high-handed . . . !" She broke off, laughing. None of it was true, of course . . . but it was a delightfully absurd fantasy. "Oh, this is too ridiculous!" she declared. "My mother is in America!" She seized on the one known fact that made his claims too preposterous for belief.

"*Was* in America," he amended smoothly. "I tracked her down and persuaded her to take the first available plane home . . . I needed her, you see. A girl likes to be married from her own

home and with her family about her
. . . and a registry office didn't really
appeal to me, either. Not binding
enough, somehow — and I want to
enjoy you for the rest of my life. So
it had to be a church wedding . . . and
why not a white wedding with all the
trimmings that a woman loves? Your
mother is a very wonderful woman,
Georgina . . . a born organiser! And
of course she quite understood that it
was all to be very secret, that we didn't
want a lot of fuss and publicity."

"I suppose she quite understood why
it was that I didn't ask her to make all
the arrangements, too," Georgina said
caustically, confident that she must
have thrown him with her quick grasp
of the absurdity of the situation.

"Laryngitis," he said promptly. "Lost
your voice completely . . . but fortunately
it will have returned in time for you to
say 'I do'." He turned to her, able to
ignore the demands of motoring for a
moment or two because of the traffic
lights that held them at a standstill.

"Darling, you'll be a very beautiful bride," he said softly and his voice was deep with love and there was much tenderness in his dark eyes.

"I don't believe a word of it," she said but reluctant laughter was tugging at her lips and dancing in her eyes . . . and there was more, much more than amusement in the depths of those eyes that met his own so candidly. It was all a dream, of course, she decided . . . a crazy, mixed-up dream like that other one, so vivid that she still recalled it, when she had walked backwards down the aisle in his shirt carrying a photo of Prudence instead of a bouquet. This dream was even more confusing with its sharp overtones of reality . . . but obviously it was only a dream. So if it was just a dream why not lie back and enjoy it! "It sounds too unlikely, you know. Bart, I think you'd better turn the car round and take me back to London."

"Don't you want to marry me?" he asked quietly.

Georgina hesitated . . . and was lost. Of course she wanted to marry him. She wanted it with all her heart. But she was not ready to commit herself just yet. "Prudence . . . ?" she said slowly.

"Delighted," he assured her truthfully. "She thinks you will be the perfect wife for me — and so do I, my darling." He smiled at her tenderly.

She was silent for a moment. Then she said carefully: "I'm still engaged to Rennie Bruce." She fingered the gold ring on her hand which had weighed so heavily on her heart.

"No, you're not," he corrected confidently. "I sent him a telegram in your name . . . thought I'd save you the trouble." He looked briefly at her hands. "You'll have to return that ring, of course. But it was inevitable, Georgina. He wasn't the man for you and I daresay you've known it for some time. I'm sorry for Bruce and I arranged some small consolation for him with the part of *Reingold*. He'll be so busy with rehearsals for the next few weeks that he'll scarcely have time to miss you."

A little bemused, Georgina withdrew Rennie's ring from her finger and dropped it inside her bag. "Is there anything you've forgotten?" she asked, a little drily.

Bart swung the car into the kerb and brought it to a halt. Then he turned to Georgina and cradled her lovely face in his strong, tender hands. "To tell you that I love you very much," he said quietly and very convincingly. He kissed her, his lips warm and tender and infinitely loving. "And to ask if you'll marry me," he added with a little twinkle in his eyes.

She nodded, her own eyes dancing with delight because all the arrangements had been made before he proposed to her . . . it was an upside-down affair but then her world had been upside-down ever since she first knew that she loved him. "Yes, please," she said demurely and surrendered to the promise of lasting happiness that was in his kiss.

THE END

A YOUNG MAN'S FANCY
Nancy Bell

Six people get together for reasons of their own, and the result is one of misunderstanding, suspicion and mounting tension.

THE WISDOM OF LOVE
Janey Blair

Barbie meets Louis and receives flattering proposals, but her reawakened affection for Jonah develops into an overwhelming passion.

MIRAGE IN THE MOONLIGHT
Mandy Brown

En route to an island to be secretary to a multi-millionaire, Heather's stubborn loyalty to her former flatmate plunges her into a grim hazard.

WITH SOMEBODY ELSE
Theresa Charles

Rosamond sets off for Cornwall with Hugo to meet his family, blissfully unaware of the shocks in store for her.

A SUMMER FOR STRANGERS
Claire Hamilton

Because she had lost her job, her flat and she had no money, Tabitha agreed to pose as Adam's future wife although she believed the scheme to be deceitful and cruel.

VILLA OF SINGING WATER
Angela Petron

The disquieting incidents that occurred at the Vatican and the Colosseum did not trouble Jan at first, but then they became increasingly unpleasant and alarming.

1		25		49		73	
2		26		50		74	
3		27		51		75	
4		28		52		76	
5	11/16	29		53		77	
6		30		54		78	
7		31		55		79	
8		32		56		80	
9		33		57		81	
10	.	34		58		82	
11		35		59		83	
12		36		60		84	
13		37		61		85	
14		38		62		86	
15		39		63		87	
16		40		64		88	
17		41		65		89	
18		42		66		90	
19		43		67		91	
20		44		68		92	
21		45		69		COMMUNITY SERVICES	
22		46	8||	70			
23		47		71		NPT/111	
24	4|||	48		72			

RAINBOW GOLD
Juliet Gray

Looking for love, Georgina flirted
with any man who gave her a second
glance...every man, in fact, but the
one who seemed beyond her reach.
She played with fire until he came into
her life and then she drew back from
the flame that was Bart Blair – but she
was badly burned just the same and
her heart would carry the scars for
ever.

ISBN 0-7089-7541-0

9 780708 975411 >

Linford Romance Library

SYLVIA E. KIRK

A NECESSARY MARRIAGE